CW00798881

THE SAVAGE FAE'S MATE

WILD HUNT 1

LOLA GLASS

To the books and people that don't break your heart.

ONE

THE SOUND of Christmas music playing from speakers above my head melded with the unfortunate melody produced by the wheels of my rolling trash cans. Cleaning the strip-style outlet mall was never a blast, but it was much worse at this time of year.

A cold gust of wind blew past, making me shiver and tug the hem of my beanie further down my face. It cut off my vision a bit and awkwardly smooshed my long, dirty blonde hair against my neck, but it was better than being cold.

The lights on the carousel a ways ahead of me had been left on, and the ride was still spinning slowly. The stragglers at the movie theater to my left were finally leaving, but my crew had at least another three hours of cleaning to do.

Yay.

I picked up trash as I walked past the wishing fountain that everyone and their dog tossed coins into. I wasn't one of them— didn't have a penny to spare, anyway. Living in my car didn't exactly leave me with much spending money.

"Hey, Ari," my closest work-friend called out.

I didn't bother to turn around, waving at her over my shoulder.

We couldn't have been less alike if we tried. Linsey was a rich girl, whose daddy was forcing her to work this job for a few months so she could learn how the "lower class" lived. She'd only be there one more day; it was December 21st, and she would be done on the 22nd.

And me?

This was the only job I could get.

Turns out a few years in juvie for killing the foster dad who assaulted you doesn't exactly make you look like a golden candidate for a job. Or an apartment. Or anything else, really.

"Ooh, the fountain." Linsey sighed happily as she caught up to me, not even bothering to reach out for the trash can she was supposed to be pushing. That was why we were friends—because I didn't give a shit whether she helped or not.

And she never did.

"My wish came true yesterday," she announced, brushing a strand of her thick, dark hair behind her ear. Her skin was light brown, her eyes a stunning blue, and her clothes clearly expensive.

I bit my lip to stop myself from rolling my eyes.

"Jake called me back, and we totally hooked up. It was awesome." She dug into the pocket of her fancy red coat and came up with a couple of pennies. "Come on, you need to make a wish too."

She grabbed one of my trash cans and used it to drag me toward the fountain.

"It's a waste of money," I said with a sigh, accepting the penny she handed me.

I knew from experience that she wouldn't take no for an answer. Usually, I just tossed the coin in without a second glance. The only thing wishes would do was give me false hope, which was the last thing I needed.

"It's a penny. You'll survive. Actually *try* to wish for something, and maybe it will even work." She tossed me a dirty look that said she knew exactly what I had been doing every time she handed me a penny.

Then she stepped up to the fountain and lifted the coin to her lips, murmuring her wish to the damn thing. Sometimes she really seemed her age, and sometimes, I wondered why the hell I'd been forced to grow up so fast. We were both twenty, but experience-wise, we might as well have been from different planets.

She delicately tossed her penny in, then turned and watched me expectantly.

I sighed again.

"Come on, it's not going to kill you," she teased.

Damn, I hated her positive attitude sometimes.

I dragged my thumb over the head of the penny, my gaze lingering on the fountain. It was nothing fancy, but then again, neither was I.

I didn't want to make a wish—to let myself hope.

But Linsey wasn't going to let me walk away without making at least a fraction of an effort.

So, as I tossed the penny, I murmured almost silently, "I wish for a way out."

Out of my shit-show of a life, out of living in my car, out of my dead-end job...

Out of everything.

The penny landed in the water with the tiniest plop, and I watched it sink.

A long, silent moment passed.

My heart clenched.

I shouldn't have let myself wish. Wishing could be detrimental to my—

In the blink of an eye, the water fountain exploded.

Water shot in every direction, spraying from the damn thing like it was an erupting volcano. And along with the water, came the men.

Five gigantic guys, each of them massive and scarred. They had different skin colors, different hair colors, different tattoos, and different clothing—but they all towered over me, with the kind of muscles that people didn't just *have*. Their ears were long and pointed. That, coupled with the size of them, and the way they'd burst out of the fountain, told me one thing:

They weren't human.

Or from Earth, if I had to guess.

Their chests heaved, water dripping off of them as their gazes scanned the outside hallway of the strip mall. And one by one, their attention landed on *me*.

Shit.

"Shit," Linsey squeaked.

I took one step backward, and it was like I'd broken a silent wall.

"Her," one of the men growled.

Growled, like an animal.

As one, they lunged for me.

I wasn't fast enough.

No one would've been fast enough.

In a heartbeat, one of them had me in his arms and was hauling me back into the fountain, which was still spraying water like a damned fire hydrant.

I didn't have the time—or the energy—to scream. Water sprayed me and then engulfed me.

The strong arm around my abdomen was a metal bar, dragging me under the water. The world turned, my stomach flipped, and my lungs burned.

I wondered if the inhuman men had captured me only to drown me.

But finally, when I started seeing stars, we burst back through the water.

I was set on my feet on some kind of brown sand as I sucked in air, desperate relief flooding my veins. My clothes were soaked and glued to my body, but wherever I was, it was hot enough that I was sweating rather than shivering.

I was alive, so it was fine. I'd keep telling myself that, at least.

Sure, I'd been taken into a fountain, which had apparently transported me into some other place. Maybe even another world.

And sure, I was surrounded by gigantic men who looked like they could kill me with a flick of their pinkies, but—

Okay, what the hell was I doing, trying to be positive about the situation?

I was screwed.

The men were all staring at me, so I stared back, asking, "Why did you grab me?"

There was a moment of silence.

My gaze scanned the three in front of me. The two behind me, I'd check out later.

One had bleach-blond hair that was shaved on the sides, pale skin, and was covered in black, orange, and red tattoos from neck to toe, all that inked-up skin evidenced by the colorful shorts he had on.

Another had buzzed, black hair and dark brown skin, with a few shimmering tattoos on his gigantic biceps. He wore a pair of shorts similar to the blond guy's, but in navy fabric.

A third had brown hair that was cut like most of the choir boys who'd been such dicks to me back at my high school. His skin was light with a bit of a sun-tan, and he had on a pair of tight black pants with cuts in the knees.

They all looked so... different.

I mean, massive, sure. But I'd survived a co-ed juvie long enough to know that size didn't mean a damn thing—and that meant bastards came in every shape, color, and gender.

These guys hadn't hurt me yet, so I was giving them the benefit of the doubt.

"Welcome to Vevol. We are the strongest of the seelie fae. To your people, we are the Wild Hunt," one of the men behind me said.

I turned around to see him. Giving any of them my back was dangerous, but they encircled me, so there wasn't a way around that.

Since I wasn't sure which of the men had spoken, I eyed them both.

The one on the right had tan skin, a few tattoos, and a mass of curly light brown hair tied up in a man-bun. He wore a pair of small shorts that showed a hell of a lot more than I wanted to see.

The one on the left had black hair, curly on the top and cropped close on the sides. His skin was light, and he wore a pair of black pants along with a shirt that looked like a gray muscle-tee.

"Our lake has begun the process of changing you. When it's done, you will run, and we will hunt," the dark-haired man said.

His voice was low and smooth, way sexier than it should've been considering he had kidnapped me with the rest of his seelie fae bastards.

"I will *what*?"

"Run." The man's gaze was intense, and I nearly shuddered.

"Why run?"

"Because it's Winter Solstice, and your people promised ours one of your females every year. Whichever of us catches you first will mate with you," one of the guys behind me said.

I spun back to the guys back there, my eyes narrowed and scanning the group. Once again, I didn't know which one had been talking. "Mate, meaning what?"

"Eternal companion," the choir boy dude said.

Shit.

"Like a wife?" I checked. "As in, person you spend your life with?"

"Yes." The blond guy flashed me a feral grin.

There was no way I'd be able to outrun any of these guys.

"I don't feel like I'm changing," I told him. "Can you take me back to Earth?"

"No. Even if we wanted to, the portal only opens for two minutes during the solstice every year. You're stuck with us." His eyes gleamed.

That was what I got for wishing on a damned penny that I should've kept. Hadn't pop culture taught me to be careful what I wished for? Wishing for *a way out* was practically setting myself up to be abducted when a person had luck as shitty as mine was.

"The change will be completed shortly," one of the guys told me. "Brace yourself."

Brace my—

Oh, shit.

Two

SHARP, hot pain cut through my chest, and I stumbled. All of the men stepped back—none of them reaching out to catch me before I crashed to my knees, hard.

At least it was sand beneath me instead of concrete.

I sucked in air like a drowning person while heat coursed through my body. I thought I was burning—that I was dying.

But then the heat faded.

A few minutes later, I managed to open my eyes.

"A phoenix," the guy with the bicep tattoos and buzzed hair said, folding his arms over his chest. "Mine."

"Careful, brother. You know she could belong to any of us," one of the men behind me drawled. "Type means nothing."

Type of what?

There wasn't time to ask the question aloud.

"You have until sundown, little phoenix. *Run.*" The buzzed-head guy's eyes bore into my soul.

I didn't wait for another invitation. Something about his words felt like a kick to the ass, anyway.

Without turning to check out the ocean I could hear violently crashing against the shore behind me, or the tall, skinny trees that reminded me of freakishly overgrown palm trees, I took off at a sprint into the weird forest in front of me.

My heart pounded like a freight train as I crashed through bushes, barely dodging rocks and tree trunks as I went. The trees only vaguely reminded me of the ones on Earth, the coloring of their leaves a much more vibrant green and blue than anything I knew. Their trunks were much thicker around, and they didn't have the same roughness as the ones I'd seen—they looked shiny-smooth, and were all either black, white, or the same bright colors as their leaves.

The whole place smelled really good; I was attentive enough to notice that as I ran for my damned life. It was like rain and the beach, and something fresh and light that I couldn't put my finger on.

The sun was still shining overhead, but those guys hadn't seemed like the patient type. If this was some kind of wife-hunt, they would probably be coming for me as soon as it was even *close* to sunset. I needed to make as much progress as possible, even though my whole damn mind was spinning.

To go from standing in that strip mall, tossing a penny in a fountain, to here? In a different world, on the beach and then running through the jungle?

I was reeling.

Factor in the whole wife thing, and the big old bastards who would be hunting me...

The Wild Hunt.

Hadn't I heard of that in a TV show or something? I was pretty sure it had something to do with mythology of some kind, but I wasn't sure. Maybe that was something they taught the teenagers who got to graduate high school; not the ones stuck in juvie for defending themselves from would-be rapists.

A sharp stick or rock cut up into my foot, through the massive hole in the bottom of my shoe, and I muttered a curse as I kept running.

Damn old shoes

Damn shitty job.

Damn juvie.

Damn lawyer foster dad who thought he was such a 'good person' for 'helping those in need' that he 'deserved' the 'pleasure' of raping me.

Fury coursed through my veins, urging me onward.

The Wild Hunt and seelie fae bastards could go to hell right alongside my foster dad.

I was no one's prize.

I wasn't someone they could hunt down and mate with.

They might have dragged me in from Earth, but I sure as hell wasn't about to go down without fighting. If one of them tried to do what my foster dad had, they'd sleep with the worms just like he had.

No one got to *use me*, human, or fae, or any other creature.

My anger propelled me on, and on, and on, pumping through me so hotly that I didn't notice the thick scratch marks on the trees or the glimmering bits of scale mixed in with the dirt.

WHEN THE SUN started to go down, I knew I had to find a place to rest.

I was exhausted, I was dripping in sweat, I was starving... I could've kept running anyway, but with the sun going down, I had no idea what kind of animals might come out, and no way to see when the darkness of night descended fully.

So I slowed to a fast walk, eyeing the trees around me. They had changed a little, growing thicker and sturdier-looking, but the colors were the same and the trunks still looked more like stone than wood.

When I saw a massive tree with a hole carved in its trunk that looked wide enough for me to fit inside, I slowed further before stopping and eyeing the thing.

I didn't know what I was waiting for; for a damned fairy to come flying out of the center of it?

My fists clenched, ready for a fight.

A minute passed, and then another.

No fairy.

No sign of anything, actually.

I took two steps closer, my body still tensed and waiting.

When nothing happened for another two minutes, I bent down and grabbed a rock off the dirt ground beneath me. My fingers wrapped around a hunk of some kind of smooth obsidian-looking stone, but my eyes caught on something...

Glittery?

It was a dark red color, and looked smooth, like some kind of gemstone on a ring, but bigger.

One hand tightened around the obsidian, and the other reached for the dark red thing.

It had to be a rock, didn't it?

I picked it up carefully, pinching the thin red thing between my fingers and lifting it out of the dirt like the damn thing might come to life and bite me.

It didn't come to life.

I eyed it anyway.

It was just as smooth as I had thought, formed into a diamond-like shape with three rounded corners and one flat edge where the fourth corner would've been. Unlike a rock or gemstone, it was mostly flat, only curved the tiniest bit.

Staring at the thing, I tried to come up with what it might be, but couldn't think of a damn thing.

And I needed to be running, still. Or hiding, at least.

The bastards would be coming after me soon.

I tucked the strange red thing into the pocket of my faded, ripped jeans—I'd tossed my coat and sweater into the forest shortly after I started running—and tugged the hem of my old t-shirt down.

It occurred to me as I stepped closer to the hole in the tree, that the seelie fae might be able to see in the dark. I knew nothing about them except that they looked massive and were hunting me in hopes of *mating* with me, so there was every possibility that they had some kind of supernatural abilities.

Hell, they had said that I was one of them. If they were right, maybe I would have magic of some kind too. I hadn't noticed anything while I was running, but that didn't mean the magic didn't exist. They *had* called me a phoenix.

I sure as hell wouldn't complain if I found myself getting taller and stronger, like those bastards, though. Being able to defend myself? Hell yeah.

Looking around the random bit of forest I'd stopped in, I debated my options.

Stay there, and hope they couldn't find me...

Or keep moving.

Running would be more dangerous in the dark, but it was better than being a sitting duck. So, running it was.

I tossed my obsidian rock back into the dirt and took off into the forest.

Screw waiting for one of those big bastards to show up and make me his damn wife.

My blistered feet resumed pounding the ground again, and again, and again.

I'd run for as long as I had to if it meant staying alive—and staying single.

AS THE SUN WENT DOWN, the forest seemed to come alive around me. I started hearing strange noises, from animals I undoubtedly didn't have names for.

Birds flew overhead, many of them much, much bigger than anything I'd seen back on Earth. I was thankful for the weird, vibrant trees hiding me from those bastards.

After a bit of time passed, a blast of wind hit me hard.

My head jerked back and forth as I looked around for whatever had caused it.

When I tilted my head back and peered up into the trees, my breath caught in my throat. I stumbled, then stopped altogether.

My hair whipped around my face as I gawked up at the sky.

Because above me, not all that far away, there was a *dragon*.

It was massive, its scales a glittering dark gray color that reminded me of some of the expensive cars that would fly past my Honda Civic and its faded silver paint on the freeway back at home.

I watched it soar overhead, and when it had gone far enough that I couldn't see it through the blue leaves above me, I relaxed slightly.

And tried to run faster.

It was getting darker, but my eyes seemed to be adjusting to the darkness, so I barely noticed the change in light. The colors were growing less neon and vibrant to my eyes, and I wondered if that had something to do with the way I had apparently *changed*.

I was too tired to think any more about it, though.

So, I kept running.

And didn't look back.

ONLY A FEW MINUTES after the dragon flew overhead, everything in the forest seemed to quiet down.

I eyed the trees suspiciously, as if those weird bastards could tell me what all the silence was about.

They couldn't, though.

At least, not that I knew of.

I kept running, avoiding the trees a bit more now that I'd realized there was a chance the damn things might be able to talk or even just think.

The forest grew quieter and quieter, until all I could hear were the sounds of my feet crunching the leaves.

There wasn't even any damned wind.

I pushed myself harder, ignoring the pain and stress and fear—and then skidded to a stop when one of the massive bastards from earlier stepped out from behind a tree in front of me.

THREE

"WHAT THE HELL?" I snarled at the man, my heart pounding wildly as every ounce of terror I'd ignored for the past few hours surged to the surface. "Don't touch me."

The man studied me, his gaze sort of... thoughtful.

It wasn't the tatted, blond guy with the scary grin, luckily. Or the buzzed-head bicep-tat guy, who had given me that intense stare.

The guy in front of me was the one with black hair and light skin, and the muscle tee and pants.

At least it wasn't one of the half-naked ones.

"What do you want?" I demanded, when he didn't say a damned word. "I *won't* be your mate."

He kept studying me.

It was way worse than if he'd just said something slimy.

When he finally spoke, he said, "You've almost made it. If you hadn't picked up that scale, you would've."

"Almost made it *where*?" I ripped the red thing out of my pocket and eyed it for a moment.

Scale.

Dragon scale.

I chucked the damn thing into the forest, earning a hint of a smirk from the black-haired man. Fae. Fae-man. Thing.

Whatever the hell he was.

"The Stronghold. When a woman isn't claimed during the hunt, she goes there." He nodded his head in the direction I'd been running. There was nothing visibly *there*, but it was in the direction of a mountain range that had seemed like the easiest target to run toward. "Your beast's instincts have been taking you there, I'm sure."

My *what*?

Screw this conversation.

"What will it take for you to leave me here, without touching me, so I can go to the damn Stronghold by myself?" I practically growled at the man. "A kiss? A blowjob? A punch to the nuts?"

The question earned me an amused chuckle. "Who said I was going to ask for something in exchange?"

His response caught me off guard for a moment, but I scowled at him anyway. "You're a man. Men are predictable."

His amusement died, and then his eyes darkened. I hadn't realized they were light until he took two steps and somehow closed the gap between us with just those motions.

Our bodies were only an inch apart.

My head tipped back and his tilted down as he said in a deadly voice, "I'm a *dragon*, female. You may know men, but you know nothing of me."

His fingers brushed the side of my throat, and an electric pulse rushed through me. I inhaled sharply, taking an instant step backward. "Don't touch me," I snarled at him, my voice a hell of a lot shakier than I wanted to admit.

"The Stronghold is this way." He tilted his head in the direction of the mountains. "If you'd like to avoid being claimed, we'll need to hurry."

He wasn't claiming me, then.

At least there was that.

That was a hell of a lot better than being grabbed and raped, like I'd assumed was going to happen.

My heart still pounded like crazy, though.

The man started jogging. I didn't ask how he could do so with bare feet—I doubted I wanted to know the answer. Even if I did, I didn't want to hear it from him.

I jogged with him, and ignored the fact that he was moving slowly enough for me to keep up.

As we ran, I noticed that my exhaustion seemed to have faded a little. My feet hurt less than they had earlier, too.

That must've been the adrenaline kicking in. Maybe this bastard should've found me earlier.

We jogged in silence, and I noticed that the forest around us remained just as quiet as it had gotten earlier, right after the dragon had passed.

After a few minutes, I started to accept that he wasn't going to attack me. Some men were snakes—I'd definitely seen that in juvie. You had to hold your breath around most of them.

But some of them weren't awful. He seemed like he might be one of the not-awful ones, at least for the time being. And we were running in the same direction I'd already been going, so if he was lying about where he was taking me, it wasn't like he was doing any real damage to the distance I'd put between myself and the others.

My stress and curiosity got the best of me, and after a few minutes, I asked, "Why is the forest so quiet right now?"

"The creatures around us know an apex predator when they see one," he said, as if that answered all of my questions.

"What the hell does that mean?"

His lips quirked upward, in that hint of a smirk he'd shown me earlier. "I told you, I'm a dragon. You're a phoenix, but until you've shifted, the land won't recognize you."

What the hell?

Did he mean...

"You can actually turn into a dragon? I demanded. "What color are you?"

He had to be the gray dragon I'd seen flying over my head, right?

"Quite an offensive question, but you don't mean offense," he mused.

Shit.

Time to change the subject.

"What kind of animal is a phoenix?" I checked, since I was pretty sure it was more than just the little bird I'd seen in that one Harry Potter movie years ago.

"A massive bird made of fire, earth, and liquid gold."

Damn.

"And you think I can turn into one of those?"

"I don't *think*, female. You *can* shift into the form of a phoenix, and you're just as indestructible as they are."

"Don't call me female. I'm not my damn gender," I finally shot back, after far too long of a pause.

"You haven't told me your name," he countered.

Bastard.

Clever bastard.

He had a point, though.

"Ari. Short for January." I didn't know why I tagged on that last part. He didn't need to know my full name. There was a reason I didn't go by it.

"January," he murmured, as if trying to get himself used to the name, which was a word they probably didn't have in whatever his language was. I had been able to understand them since they first appeared on Earth, which I was chalking up to whatever magic they had that could connect our two worlds, even if it only worked on Winter Solstice like they claimed.

"Do you have a name?" I asked. Maybe the question was rude, but they were a different kind of creature than I was.

"All living things have names in Vevol." He sounded amused by my question, rather than insulted, which was good. "Names have power here."

Names had some kind of power, and I'd just given him mine without a damn thought about it.

Fantastic.

"You'd better give me your name then," I huffed at him.

He chuckled. "Calian."

"Cal-ee-in," I sounded it out, testing the unfamiliar word.

"Mmhm." His murmur sounded a bit different, but I couldn't pinpoint how or what about it seemed that way. "Don't give anyone else your full name, whether male or female. Should they learn it from someone other than you, it won't harm you. But if you give it to them yourself, you give them power to call on you. Your full name should only leave your lips the first time you give it to your mate."

Power to *what*?

"That's absolutely insane," I told him, panting a little thanks to the pace I was pushing myself to keep.

There was no way Calian was his whole name. He clearly didn't want me to be his mate, so he wouldn't have given me a way to call on him, whatever that really meant.

Asshole.

"We're here. Slow down, before you—"

I slammed into something really hard, and really invisible, before I could slow down.

Curses flew from my lips as I crashed to the ground, my face aching from collision. My nose was throbbing, but my eyes weren't watering and I didn't feel any blood dripping from it at least.

"Damn you," I groaned at Calian, peeling myself off the dirt. He was kneeling beside me, a hint of a smirk on his lips as he offered me a hand.

I took it, swearing and jumping back when he shocked me again, like he had the first time we touched. "What the hell was that?" I grumbled at him, shaking my hand out and taking a couple of steps away from the guy.

He was doing his stupidly-attractive half-smirk thing again as he turned toward the invisible wall, and I didn't realize he had ignored my question until he knocked on the invisible thing I'd attacked with my face.

The sound that echoed from the rap of his fist reminded me a hell of a lot of a front door.

He stepped back after knocking, and I followed suit, rubbing at my nose. Strangely enough, it had stopped hurting already. Probably because I was a damn phoenix now.

The place he had knocked on swung open a moment later, and a woman holding a gigantic sword and wearing a fierce scowl stood in what was definitely a doorway. The door had way too many locks, though—and the thing was at least six times as thick as any other one I'd seen. Looked like it was made of solid stone, too.

Her gaze landed on me, but she didn't lower her sword. Her eyes were an unnatural bright gold, and her hair was a normal, human deep brown. Like me, she had pale skin and thin lips. "Name?"

Suddenly, I understood Calian's warning.

If a simple name could give me power over someone, or give someone power over me, that was a loaded question.

And he had set me up to protect myself.

A wave of gratitude hit me hard, though I knew better than to thank him for what he'd done. Thanking someone implied that they'd done you a favor, and that you owed them... and I didn't want to owe him.

"Ari," I said to the sword chick.

Her eyes narrowed and flashed suspiciously at Calian before looking back at me. "*Full* name."

"Ariana Faust."

The admission relaxed her slightly, though she didn't know it was a lie.

"Welcome to Vevol, Ari. I'm Ana." She reached a hand out and grabbed my arm, then unceremoniously yanked me inside the Stronghold.

The door slammed behind me, and she released my arm before quickly getting to work on the locks. "Did he touch you?" she demanded as her fingers moved deftly over the mechanisms.

The woman had clearly done this more than a few times.

"Um, not really, no."

"Good." She was halfway through all thirteen of the locks—I counted. "Lian isn't one of the worsts, but being touched by any of the seelie bastards is a good way to get yourself locked into a mating you don't want."

Did she mean being touched at all?

Because he had touched me, just barely—and twice.

And she had called him Lian, pronounced Lee-in, which was clearly a shortened version of his name.

Which meant he had given me his whole name.

Which meant...

Oh, shit.

"Bastard," I hissed between my teeth.

"What?" She shot me a demanding look. The woman didn't seem to have any other settings besides suspicious and demanding.

"He did touch me—twice. It felt like getting electrocuted. And he said his name was Calian."

Her expression twisted into a grimace. "You're screwed."

After turning, she spun and started walking down the hallway a hell of a lot faster than I expected.

I had to jog to keep up with her. "Does it mean what I think it means?"

"That he's decided you're his mate? Yes." She didn't bother glancing at me. "We'll throw you a funeral when you're gone."

My eyebrows shot upward as she led me into a large room full of couches, books, and strange-looking screens that sort of reminded me of TVs. "He's going to *kill* me? I thought it was like marriage."

"We call them funerals because they're the end of your humanity," another woman chirped.

My attention jerked toward her, and I found her curled up on a couch off to the side of the room. She held a book in her hands, and a soft-looking blanket was draped over her legs. She wore a sweatshirt and a pair of fuzzy socks, along with what looked like leggings from what I could see. Her curly black hair was up in a puff on top of her head, and her expression was a hell of a lot more relaxed than Ana's. Her skin was dark brown, and her eyes soft hazel.

At least she looked comfortable. That meant the Stronghold wasn't a prison.

"What? I thought we all change when we get here," I argued. "They said I'm a phoenix."

"Yep, we can all shift into a legendary beast form like they can. You won't transform until you've bonded with your mate or been taken to the unseelie half of the world, though, and you have to last five years here to make it to the unseelies. If Lian has decided you're his mate, I doubt you'll make it one."

Shit, this was a lot to take in.

"What's your name?" the laid-back woman checked.

Lie again, my instincts practically screamed.

I'd never really played well with others.

I didn't need to lie, though. My nickname—which I did actually go by, ninety-nine percent of the time—was enough.

"Ari. What about you?"

Considering the power of names, I felt like I needed to ask, not just assume she would give it to me.

"Mare, if we're only swapping nicknames." She gave me a quick wink. "I don't blame you for wanting to keep your full name quiet. The only person I told mine to was Ana, but she's been running this place for five years now."

Five years?

I glanced back at her. "I thought you said the unseelie take you after five years."

"They do. I'll be leaving tonight," Ana admitted, her expression a bit stiff.

Damn, no wonder she was so angry.

Or maybe that was just her personality. I wouldn't blame her either way.

"How are the unseelies different?" I asked.

"We don't really know." Mare shrugged on the couch. "We try not to talk to the fae guys very often, so we don't give them the wrong idea, but we haven't met the unseelies."

"How many of you are there?" I checked, looking around the room. No one else was hiding, as far as I could see.

"Five, right now. The fae are getting anxious about it, too. Usually one of them finds a mate every two or three years—we made it five. Looks like you're going to break the streak." Ana didn't sound thrilled about that, either.

"Where are the others?"

"Dots and Sunny are setting up for my funeral. North is asleep, probably. She keeps weird hours, and avoids us." Ana shrugged. "Things are pretty chill here. Or they were, until you showed up."

So this would've been a helluva place to be, if Calian hadn't touched me and told me his full name.

Great.

Just my damn luck.

"You won't have a room until Ana leaves, but you can borrow mine to shower in," Mare offered. "You don't want to miss it when the unseelie show up, but you have an hour or two, I'd guess."

I glanced down at myself.

Shit, I had forgotten what bad shape I was in. I was a damned wreck.

I looked back up and jerked my head in a nod.

"That would be great, thanks."

"I'm at the end of the hallway, on the left. Door has my name on it, can't miss it." She winked at me.

I nodded again, stepping up and slipping down the hall.

Damn, my brain was spinning.

FOUR

I SPENT LONGER in the shower than I probably should've, but it was the first time since I'd been out of juvie that I didn't need to rush through a shower at the cheap gym I'd joined for that purpose. I hadn't realized how much anxiety had revolved around showering until I was behind a locked door, my shoulders relaxing under the hot stream.

My feet weren't blistered, despite the terrible pain I'd had for part of the time while I was running, and my muscles weren't sore. I wasn't even hungry anymore. And though I was tired, it wasn't the shaky-legged exhaustion I would've been feeling if I was still human.

Damn, it was cool to be fae.

Despite my initial horror of being transported to a new world and told to run for my life before some bastard caught me and turned me into his mate somehow, I was feeling sort of... positive about my experience thus far.

I was alive.

I was safe.

I wasn't living in my car anymore.

There was no more record of juvenile detention or murder on my shoulders.

No one to refuse me an apartment or a job because of what I'd done to my bastard of a foster dad.

No more Earth to remind me of the shitty hand life had dealt me.

In Vevol, I was just Ari.

Sure, I had given a fae dude my full name, which was probably a terrible decision, but it hadn't come back to bite me in the ass yet. It probably would, but for now, everything was actually kind of great.

I needed to watch myself, though, because I had a terrible tendency to get all hopeful right before everything turned to shit and then burned me to a crisp right afterward.

My mind wandered back to the strange forest, with Calian.

He had said that a person's full name was a way to call on them, whatever the hell that meant.

I was sure it wasn't something magical—at least, I was pretty sure.

I considered trying it out by saying his name while focusing on trying to call him to me, but decided against it until I could ask one of the other girls about it. Although, they might not actually know. It sounded like none of them had ever hooked up with the seelie fae dudes in the time they'd been there, so they might not know nitty gritty details like that.

Hmm.

Now I was getting curious.

Curiosity was a shitty quality, though. It only ever led to disappointment or horror.

I shampooed my hair vigorously, trying to tamp down that stupid curiosity. I didn't understand a damn thing about the power of names; trying it out would be absolutely stupid as hell.

But that didn't mean I didn't want to try it.

I conditioned my hair quickly. The shower, shampoo, and razor all looked like our normal earth-style shit, which made me feel a little more comfortable. Not that I required comfort to shower, or function, or do anything else important. I excelled at doing uncomfortable things while living in discomfort.

It was a shitty fact, but a fact nonetheless.

Knowing I needed to get out before I did something really, terribly stupid, I rinsed my hair and then turned off the water.

After I dried off, I wrapped the thick, white towel around myself and stepped out of the room, holding onto the thing tightly.

Wearing a towel was one of the prime times a person could get attacked. Any vulnerability was a weakness that a girl like me just couldn't afford.

My gaze swept the room.

Empty, still.

And the door was shut.

My shoulders relaxed slightly.

What if I really was safe there?

What if I could just... live?

If that was the case, I was really damn grateful for the penny Linsey had practically forced me to take.

A knock sounded on the door, and I tensed.

"I left clothes for you on the bed," Mare called from outside the room. "Feel free to use my brush, bandages, and anything else you might need. It's in the bathroom, and the fae supply all of it."

"Thank you," I called back, ignoring the panic that had swollen in my chest.

I was still fine.

The door to the bedroom hadn't been locked when I went in to take a shower—I hadn't wanted to piss Mare off when she was being kind to me. So, it wasn't surprising that she'd been able to come into the room. That was fine.

I was fine.

Shit, I hated being vulnerable though.

I crossed the room and quickly locked the door.

Getting dressed in the soft, sturdy leggings and oversized sweatshirt calmed me down a bit. I was built thicker than Mare was, so everything was a bit tight, but I was used to that after a childhood full of thrift-store clothing.

Back in the bathroom, I tugged a brush through my hair. Unlike the clothing, it didn't look like it was from Earth. The bristles were strange, and the handle was made out of the white, stone-looking wood I'd seen so much of in the forest. It felt odd against my fingertips, but not uncomfortably so.

I looked through the rest of the cupboards, checking for anything that might possibly be suspicious. When I didn't find anything, it didn't make me more comfortable. If anything, it just reminded me to wait for the next pin to drop.

Fully dressed, with my hair combed and my feet bare, I padded out of the room a couple of minutes later. Mare shot me a quick smile from her seat on the couch. Ana was eating something that looked suspiciously like cake, sitting beside three girls I didn't recognize. I waved at them, and they waved back.

Not feeling like I was in the mood to socialize, even for the possibility of cake, I headed over to the couch where Mare was sitting. I wouldn't sit next to her—didn't want to annoy her—but she felt safer than the other girls, so I'd stick with her.

Though I didn't want to read, I pretended to scan the books on the shelf. I had a shitty case of dyslexia that made it difficult to read at all, and while I could push through it when I wanted to, I had no desire to do so at the moment.

What I really wanted was a nap, but I wasn't going to get that. Not until I had a room of my own, with a lockable door. A place to feel safe.

I would've given anything for that back on Earth. I'd just have to embrace it for as long as I had it now that I was in Vevol.

I grabbed a book and sat down. Opening to the first page, I stared at the words. I was skilled at pretending to read—people reading books seemed laid-back and unconfrontational, which were two very good traits to possess in juvie.

So I *read*.

And silently watched everyone interact.

I only had two minutes to study them before there was a knock on the gigantic door.

All four of the other girls went silent.

"It's time," one of the ones I didn't know murmured.

"Dammit." Ana sighed, tucking her hands into the pockets of her jeans. I noticed that she had cleaned up and changed. My gaze followed her as she grabbed a backpack that I hadn't noticed sitting on the floor by her feet.

"It's going to be great," one of the girls promised.

"It's going to be hell," another one grumbled.

"I'm going to survive, which is what counts," Ana shot back at both of them. "And so are you. Don't touch the guys, don't let them touch you. I'll see you when your time is up here, okay?" She looked around the room, and her gaze made it back to Mare, and then stopped on me. "Good luck, newbie."

I shrugged back.

No point in thanking her for wishing me luck. Luck had never been what kept me alive.

If she was going to wish me something, I'd rather she wish me good food and a safe place to rest my head.

The person at the door knocked again, louder.

"The seelie won't wait—but the unseelie will," Ana murmured, as she started across the room. "Remember that. The seelie are the wild ones—there's no control here."

Shit, I liked the sound of that.

No control.

No power-obsessed bastards who thought they could own you.

No one to figuratively hold you by the tits or the throat.

I'd take a fist fight over a verbal battle any day of the week.

Everyone followed Ana to the door, myself included, though I trailed behind at the back of the group. Mare walked beside me, not leaving me behind.

"Who's next?" I murmured to her.

"Me," she admitted, her gaze a bit wistful. "I've been hoping for a seelie fae to come knocking at the door for me, but it hasn't happened. Something about the unseelies just seems... cold. You'll see, when one of them shows up for Ana. The other girls prefer that, but... not me."

I nodded, my damned curiosity flaring a bit.

The safer I felt, the more the ridiculous character trait seemed to grate on me.

"REMEMBER, always answer with a weapon pointed at the fae," Ana warned us, as she began undoing the locks. "Don't accept invitations from fae who haven't been camped outside for more than three months. Trust each other—and no one else."

Damn, that sounded like a shitty way to live.

Then again, I lived by most of those rules myself. So I couldn't exactly argue.

"Don't worry about me," she added. "I'll screw up any fae who tries to touch me, seelie or unseelie. I'll see you ladies soon."

With that, she pulled the door the rest of the way open.

There was a knife in her hand, though—keeping the fae away from her.

"Ana," a familiar voice drawled.

My body tensed.

Calian.

"Lovely to see you again. Let me introduce my friend, Druze."
Calian gestured toward a man beside him. He was just as tall as
Calian and the other gigantic fae I'd met, but had short, wavy
blond hair, pale skin, and was wearing something that resembled
office clothing back on Earth—a button-down shirt, and pants
that resembled slacks.

"Basilisk," Ana hissed at the man.

His lips curved upward wickedly. "Pretty little human." He said
the last word like it disgusted him.

Ana muttered something that sounded suspiciously like, "I wish,"
but the man's gaze had already lifted to the rest of us, and was
slowly dragging over our group. Something about the intensity of
his gaze as it landed on me made me shudder slightly.

"Brother." Calian's voice was clipped as he smacked the basilisk
dude on the back. "Eyes off that one. January is mine."

The basilisk's gaze skidded to Calian, flooded with interest.

I didn't hear whatever he said to Calian—the words *January is
mine* were thundering too loudly in my mind.

The other girls' gazes jerked to me, and I felt my face reddening.

They couldn't use my full name against me since I hadn't given it
to them myself, if Calian was to be believed. But still, having it
spoken aloud made me feel sort of... naked.

Vulnerable.

My defenses rose, and I stared at the basilisk man because
suddenly, he was the safest target for my eyes.

Screw Calian.

Screw everyone.

I could do it; I could ignore him for five damn years for the sake of getting away from the bastard.

He had lied to me and claimed me like I was a damn loaf of bread, and touched me.

The bastard deserved to be ignored for five years, and then abandoned. He could try his luck with some other poor human chick.

I was not his *anything*.

"Shall we?" the basilisk drawled to Ana, holding out his elbow.

"I'm not touching you," she growled back, shoving her knife at him. He took a smooth step backward and she filled the space he left, using it to slide past him.

Damn, I kind of wanted to be Ana.

Angry, kick-ass, and confident?

Sign me up.

"Ladies." The basilisk guy nodded at us. "I'll see you soon."

His gaze lingered on me before he turned around.

Shit, I hated how his eyes felt on me.

I definitely did not want to see him soon.

But if I wanted to get away from the seelie, I would have to.

Dammit, why couldn't there be an easy, good alternative? Maybe a magical castle where I could be single and alone, with my own space, food, and clothing, for the rest of my life?

Despite Ana's warning, the girl who replaced her in the doorway didn't have a weapon in her hand.

"I request entrance," Calian said smoothly, after Ana and the basilisk guy were gone.

"Fuck off." The girl in the doorway shut the thick stone slab in his face, hard.

I almost felt bad for the guy.

Almost.

FIVE

ALL OF THE girls were looking at me when they turned away from the door.

"January, huh?" one of them asked.

My cheeks flushed a bit. "Didn't give myself that name, if that's what you're asking."

"I like it," Mare remarked. "I wish I could get my actual name out in the open, honestly. Lian did you a favor, even if you don't realize it now."

My face heated further. "His name is Calian."

"Even hotter than Lian, somehow," one of the girls muttered.

"Lucky bitch," another one of them sighed dramatically. My gaze flicked to her, and lingered. She was the one who had been in the doorway, and my eyes widened slightly when I saw her, only because she looked so much less human than the rest of us. "I'm Sunny," she offered. Her hair was black at the roots but faded to gray, and then white by the time it reached the ends. She'd pulled it up into two puffs on top of her head, reminding me of the space buns that had been in style when I was in high school, which I'd never been brave enough to try. Her skin was dark brown, and her lips were painted black. One of her eyes was silver while the other was the same shade as her lips.

My face was burning when I realized I'd been staring.

Staring could get a girl shanked.

"It's okay, I'm used to it." She shrugged. "I'd stare at you if you were as stunning as I am." She gave a little half-twirl that made me snort.

"Some of our appearances seem to be more affected by the magic than others," another girl said. "I've got this massive tattoo over my back and arm. It appeared a few weeks after I got here." Her skin was the same pale shade as mine, but she had more freckles than I knew was possible. Her hair was a bright golden color that mine sure as hell didn't resemble, even though the colors probably belonged to the same family. Mine was a solid dirty-looking blonde.

"I'm Dots, by the way."

"I've always wanted a tattoo," I admitted. "Never had the money."

"Maybe you'll get lucky with the magic, then," she suggested.

"Unlikely." The last girl whose name I didn't know pushed past me. "Good luck with the king, dead girl." I didn't get a great look at her, but from what I could see, she was pale and thin. She was wearing a high-necked long-sleeve shirt, as well as leggings and socks. With her long, thick black hair swaying around her face, I barely saw an inch of her skin.

"That's North. Don't let her offend you; she just hates being here. She hated Earth too, though. She's a hellhound and has patches of burnt-looking skin everywhere her scars used to be. She had a *lot* of scars," Dots explained in a hushed voice.

Damn, I hoped they didn't always gossip like this. I shuddered to think what they'd say about me.

I'd be on board with burn marks, though. At least then, my appearance would tell people to back off without me saying any actual words.

"None of us had good lives, back on Earth," Mare murmured. "I'm sure you were in a shitty boat too. For some of us, this is the second chance we always hoped for. For others, it's another hell. You get to choose how you see it."

She looped her arm through mine, and the sudden touch made me jerk a bit.

It wasn't terrible, though.

It was actually kind of... nice.

How long had it been since anyone touched me?

Other than Calian, who I hadn't wanted to touch me?

How long had it been since I actually sort of trusted someone?

I didn't want to think about that.

"Come on, let's get you settled in your new room. Ana went crazy with the cleaning spray while you were gone. As suspicious as that girl is about everything, she never hesitated to do her part around here," Mare said cheerfully, tugging me down the hallway by my arm.

"I'm going to miss that crazy bitch," Sunny remarked, as she and Dots walked alongside me.

The fact that they were going to miss her told me plenty about her. She might have been a little insane, but she had to have been a decent friend—because there were very, very few people that had ever treated me well enough for me to actually miss them after they were out of my life.

Then again, I'd grown up the grumpy, sad girl in the foster system. I wasn't one of the cute little ones who bounced back from the shit they went through and found forever homes—I was one of the temperamental ones who moved around and never found her place.

Maybe now that I was out, and free, that would change.

As long as I could stay away from Calian, that was.

"Here we are," Dots announced with a flourish of her hand. "Home sweet home. It's nothing fancy, but definitely a hell of a lot more comfortable than the forest outside."

"Amen to that," Sunny muttered.

"The fae will bring clothes, food, and other supplies for you over the next few weeks. They usually drag it out so they have an excuse for us to let them in, so more of the men can meet us. Although none of us have ever been claimed by one of them, so I'm not sure how that will affect it..." Dots trailed off, her expression contemplative.

"How do they convince you to let them in?" I asked, curiosity getting the better of me again.

"The bastards aren't stupid. They know we're suckers for good foods, new movies, new books, new clothes... anything we don't have access to in here already. We're well-stocked with the basics, this world's version of beans, rice, and enough spices to make it taste good. But I'll be damned if their chocolate cake doesn't make my mouth water just thinking about it," Sunny said with a grin.

"It's been a few weeks since the last fae bribed us for a meeting. Ana made them wait outside for a month before she'd let any of us talk to them. Now that she's gone, and you've got a fae on your ass, hopefully we'll have more of their desserts."

I could definitely see where she was coming from with that. Hell, maybe I agreed.

For a whole damn chocolate cake, I could put up with a hell of a lot.

Then again, accepting a chocolate cake from Calian would probably give him an idea I didn't want him to have. So, I'd have to think hard before I accepted anything from him.

"So how did all of you make it here without one of them catching you?" I wondered as I walked around the room. None of them seemed like they were in a hurry to leave, or like they were judging me for checking for anything that might resemble a weapon or a hidden camera.

"Oh, the hunt is just a big theatrical thing. They need you to move fast for it to work the way it should. Assuming you jog for most of the time before the sun sets, you'll reach the Stronghold before any of them can make your scent out. The ocean washes it away well enough that only a fae who's a compatible mate will be able to smell you well enough to track you."

What the hell?

Calian has said it was because I picked up the scale—not because he could smell me.

Which was another damned lie.

That bastard could take a hike.

No way in hell was I going to let him make me his mate.

"Well, I'm going to start on dinner. Go ahead and make yourself at home, even though you don't have much yet. I'm sure Lian will be back with some stuff for you soon enough," Mare said cheerfully.

She and the others left me to my room.

It was pretty much bare—no clothes in the square, walk-in closet. No blankets on the mattress, though it still looked a hell of a lot more comfortable than the back seat of my car, which was where I had been sleeping for nearly a year. No toiletries in the bathroom, no shampoo in the shower, no comb in the drawers, which seemed to be styled to look like the ones we'd had back on earth.

It was still the best place I'd lived in almost a decade.

For a couple of minutes, I sat on the bed—which was ridiculously comfortable—mentally going over everything that had happened.

Then my stomach growled, and with a sigh, I stood.

It was time to eat, and then face the fae who thought I was his, whenever he showed up with more stuff for me.

DINNER WAS FUN, to be honest. The girls were chatty, but not annoyingly so. North didn't make an appearance, but Sunny got her to open the door long enough to take her portion of the food —and there was plenty of food.

It wasn't awkward.

I even found myself looking forward to the next meal when it was over.

Mare turned on a movie while we all cleaned up, and we were done in time to get cozy on the couch when it started. The action was so foreign to me, but a happy warmth spread in my chest that I hoped would never leave.

And there I was, hoping again even though I knew I shouldn't.

Oh well.

I could enjoy the fun while it lasted.

PARTWAY INTO THE MOVIE—AN action film I had never seen —there was a loud knock on our massive door.

Four grins turned my way.

"If he has chocolate cake, give him whatever he wants," Sunny told me.

I rolled my eyes at her, but...

Chocolate cake sounded really damn good.

"Do I really need to open the door with a weapon?" I asked them as I slipped off the couch. They paused the movie for me, which was really damn nice. I couldn't say I'd ever had friends who would pause a movie for me before.

"Nah. The fae don't have any women of their own, so hurting one of us is worse than a death sentence. Bastards might try to touch your arms or face or something, but never go further than that," Sunny said.

Her words comforted me, to be honest.

Though I was kind of shocked they didn't have any women of their own, I guessed it kind of made sense according to what I did know.

Why would they bother taking women from Earth if they could find mates among their own people?

I felt slightly more comfortable than I expected to as I walked to the door.

Six

It took me a lot longer to open all those damn locks than it had taken Ana. The fae on the other side of the door waited patiently, probably hearing me working on the stupid things.

When I finally wrenched the door open, I found myself face-to-face with Calian. I hated the way my breath caught in my throat at the size of him, and the power I could sort of feel swirling around him.

"Hello." His lips curved up in a half-smirk.

The same one from the jungle that made me want to punch him.

I ignored the urge though, because there was a duffel bag hanging off his shoulder, and he was holding a cake in his hands. It didn't look like chocolate, but cake was cake.

"I'm not your possession," I told him flatly. "And you already lied to me multiple times, so I'm not interested."

"I never lied to you," he corrected me. "And I'm very much aware that you don't belong to me yet."

Yet.

That bastard.

I started to shut the door in his face, but he caught it easily with a foot planted in the door's way.

"You need these." He tugged the duffel bag's strap off his shoulder with the hand that wasn't holding the cake, and carefully maneuvered it past me, setting it on the ground. "And this." He smoothly placed the edge of the cake's platter against my abdomen. None of the frosting got on my sweatshirt, and my hand automatically lifted to cradle the mouthwatering dessert.

"How can you possibly think you didn't lie to me?" I finally recovered and snapped at him when he lowered his hand off the door. And dammit, I didn't shut the thing. "You bluntly told me that I needed to get to the stronghold or I would find myself mated."

He dipped his head in a nod, still wearing that damned smirk. "Mated to *me*. I only have so much control, woman."

I blinked at him.

Who the hell was this guy?

His smirk morphed into a full-out grin when my eyes narrowed. "And the scale?"

"I would've watched you make it here from afar if you hadn't picked it up. Seeing another man's scale in your hand forced the beast in me to react." He shrugged slightly.

"Are scales special?" I demanded.

"No. We shed them the same way we shed hair."

Then why the hell did he care that I was holding someone else's?

"You asked me for my name," I argued, though my anger was sort of… losing steam.

"I'll need it at some point."

"And you seriously gave me your real name?" My voice was raising, flooded with frustration.

"It's yours to use any moment you wish to see me," he agreed, that damn smirk back in place. "Preferably while you're naked."

Bastard.

I resisted the urge to smash the cake in his gorgeous face.

That would be a sad, sad waste of cake.

"I'm not going to do that," I shot back.

He was still smirking.

Damn him.

Damn him straight to whatever this world's version of hell was.

"I'll collect more of the items you need and bring them by in the morning. Different groups produce different things, so it'll take some legwork. Luckily for you, I have great legs."

"You have wings," I shot back.

His smirk curved into a wicked grin. "Glad you noticed."

With that, he turned and strode away.

I slammed the door to stop myself from staring at his incredible ass.

My fingers struggled with the locks one-handed, but Dots walked up and took over.

"What did you have to do for the cake?" she checked.

"I'm surprised you guys didn't listen in," I grumbled.

She flashed me an amused smile. "Ana would've, but we're not into that. If you want to hook up with the sexy fae, that's totally your call."

I heaved a sigh. "He didn't ask me to do anything; just handed the damn thing over. Said I needed it. Maybe he thinks I'm too skinny or something."

"Answering the door was enough this time," Dots mused as she finished the last of the locks. "Next time, it won't be so easy."

Great.

"We'd better enjoy this cake then, because it's the last one we're going to have for a while."

She laughed. "That's the spirit. Welcome to Vevol, and all that." She winked at me, grabbing the duffel bag and tossing it over her shoulder.

My stomach clenched at the way she picked my things up without so much as asking permission. I had to force myself to follow her without starting a fight in an attempt to get it back.

Not everyone was so panicky when it came to holding on to their possessions.

I stood in the doorway while Dots set it just inside the doorway of my room, then shut the door behind her.

"I'm surprised you guys don't split everything," I said, relaxing slightly now that my things were in my room, as safe as they could be for the time being.

"Whatever you get from the fae is rightfully yours. If you don't want to share, you don't share. Even when it comes to cake." She shrugged a bit and walked beside me as I headed toward the kitchen. "I kissed one of them for a tub of their version of ice cream. So damn worth it. Because I shared, the other girls also shared their food whenever they got it from one of the fae who came to meet them. That's usually how it works around here."

Damn.

I kind of loved that.

"Whatever you do, don't touch North's shit. She's not into sharing," Dots warned.

I could understand that, too.

Maybe I'd bring her a slice of cake as a peace offering.

Or maybe not. It would probably depend on how good the cake was.

When we got to the kitchen, though, the curiosity in me won out. I wanted to see what would happen with North if I brought her something without expecting her to reciprocate. I had been the prickly bitch enough times to know that there was always a reason —and that it was just a defense mechanism.

So, I halved the cake and cut it into five pieces, saving some for tomorrow. I'd probably need the sugar to cheer myself up after I turned down whatever the hell Calian asked for in exchange for the next treat he brought me. Especially if it was the fae version of ice cream; I was a damned sucker when it came to ice cream.

After giving three pieces to Dots so she could distribute them, I carried my cake and North's over to her door, then knocked on it.

"Fuck off," she yelled in response.

I fought a grin.

How many times had that been my answer to people trying to talk to me?

Pretty much every damn time when I was a teenager.

"I brought you cake. Not sure what flavor it is, but it's sort of a cream color. Smells incredible," I called out. "No expectations come with it. It's just cake."

There was a moment of silence, and then the door was ripped open. Gorgeous, reddish-gold eyes glared back at me. "Everything has a price," she growled at me.

The other girls said you couldn't shift until you found a mate or went to live with the unseelies, but smoke was definitely curling off of North, as if she was on fire or was about to catch on fire.

"I know. I grew up in foster care. Went to juvie at fifteen after killing one of my temporary parents. Nothing on Earth is free, and I'm sure Vevol is the same. But I paid the price for the damned cake, and all it cost you was a little chat in your doorway." I put the plate against her abdomen, like Calian had done to me, and hid my tendril of amusement when her arm lifted to cradle it the same way mine had. "I'm Ari, and I'm not dead just because some fae bastard thinks I'm going to be his wife."

With that, I turned and walked away.

I felt her gaze on my back, but it wasn't anywhere near the first time that had happened.

People always stared.

When it bothered me, I'd stare right back.

None of the other girls commented on me giving cake to North when I sat back down on the couch. We started the movie again, and my body slowly relaxed.

Watching the movie with them felt... nice.

Hell, maybe it even felt happy.

I wasn't going to let myself think too much about that though, because happiness was always ripped away after I acknowledged it.

After the movie was over, Dots volunteered to do the dishes as a thank-you to me for sharing my cake, and I didn't disagree. I was the one who had to deal with the fae bastard who might be a little obsessed with me, even if he hadn't actually lied to me.

I was still pretty pissed about his reasoning behind what he'd said, though. That he couldn't have controlled himself forever, and I was in danger of getting mated if I'd stayed in the forest with him.

Especially the part where scales were basically strands of hair, and he got possessive when I picked up someone else's.

He had to be the gray dragon, I decided, as I walked back to my room to see what I had in my new duffel bag. I would give Mare back her clothes, too, because I didn't know who she'd needed to talk to in order to get them. I didn't want to disrupt the balance of sharing that the women in the Stronghold had, and I sure as hell didn't want to owe Mare anything.

Back in my room, I grabbed the duffel bag by the strap and carried it to the mattress, setting it down kind of carefully since I didn't know what was in it or if anything was breakable.

The zipper looked a bit different than the ones I was used to, but it was easy to work, so I had the bag open a moment later.

On top, there was a pile of fabric, so I pulled it out of the bag. When I quickly realized that it was a thick and ridiculously-soft blanket, I hugged it to my chest, inhaling the fabric deeply. It smelled fresh and light, like the forest had when I'd run through it, and I loved it.

I was never letting that thing go if I could help it.

The blanket was placed carefully on the bed, and I pulled out the next thing—a thin, smooth bundle of fabric that reminded me of a sheet. The texture was slightly different than what I was used to, and it was shaped like a big pillowcase instead of elastic-lined, but I didn't hesitate to wrestle it onto my mattress. When it was on securely, I draped my blanket over it, and then let my gaze sweep up and down the bed.

It was already more welcoming than any other one I'd ever used.

I loved it.

Returning to the duffel bag, I pulled out a pillow. It was squishier than any I'd used before, the texture softer but also thicker somehow. I put that at the head of my bed and fought to ignore the happiness swelling in my chest again.

No acknowledging happiness.

Happiness only ever led to shit falling apart.

Back at the duffel bag, I found bottles of shampoo and conditioner. They smelled more manly than Mare's, but not in a way I disliked. The scent actually kind of reminded me of the way the blanket and pillow smelled.

There were a few other simple toiletries in the duffel, and when I had them all put away in the bathroom, I returned to the bag.

And then stared down inside it.

I blinked once at the final thing inside, and then again.

When I reached inside, I had to bite my lip hard.

My fingers slid over the large, glittering, dark gray scale.

I should've left it in the bag, but something within me wouldn't allow it. Honestly, I was fascinated by it. By the magic of this world I'd been dragged into, by the fact that a man—even if he was technically a fae man—could transform into an actual dragon.

I had seen him flying over me; I knew he was real.

And that meant the world was real too, as insane as everything was.

Despite its insanity, I wanted it all to be real so badly that it hurt.

I tucked the scale into the fabric case that my pillow had come wrapped in, then stripped off my borrowed clothing and tucked myself under the insanely-soft blanket. I wasn't going to sleep in Mare's clothes—they were hers, and I didn't want to wreck them in any way since I'd be returning them as soon as I had some of my own.

Theoretically, I would have some of my own in the very near future. Calian had said he'd be back in the morning.

So, I tugged the blanket up to my chin, not expecting to fall asleep quickly. But with the delicious scent in my nose and the gentle pressure of the heavy, soft blanket on my bare skin, I was out almost instantly.

SEVEN

A SOFT KNOCK at my new bedroom door woke me up the next morning. A semi-familiar voice called out, "January, there's a fae here for you."

It took me a minute to stumble out of bed, remember where I was, and why there was a fae there for me. I threw on the clothes I'd borrowed from Mare the day before while I struggled through my exhausted thoughts.

When I opened the door, a cheerful-looking Mare stood outside my room, fully dressed. Her curls were down and gorgeous, and I blinked at her a couple of times until she pointed me toward the front door.

I quickly made it to the door and struggled through all of the locks before tugging the door open.

Calian's expression was hard as I opened it, but it softened as his gaze trailed up and down my figure.

That was weird, but whatever.

"What?" I asked him, eyeing the bag over his shoulder. It was at least twice as big as the one from the day before, and for the life of me, I couldn't guess what he could've possibly put in there. No way in hell did I need that many clothes, and clothes were pretty much all I was missing.

"You look calm," he told me.

I blinked at him.

His lips curved upward just the tiniest bit.

I noticed circles under his eyes.

"I thought you said you'd have to go to multiple places to get everything else you thought I'd need," I told him.

"I did." He easily lifted the bag off his shoulder and pretty much tossed it into the room behind me.

"So you lied?" I checked.

His eyes narrowed. "Why do you keep assuming I'd lie to you?"

"I assume everyone will lie to me," I shot back. "And you definitely didn't answer my question."

His eyes narrowed further. "I said I'd need to go to multiple places. During the night, I flew to those places, collecting your things. Now, I'm here." He gestured to the huge bag. "And so are your things."

I blinked. "You didn't sleep?"

"I can sleep while I'm waiting out here to convince you to consider me as your mate." He gestured to a place along the stronghold's invisible wall. I noticed what looked like a tent built up against it.

Damn.

Ana must've really made the fae men camp out for a month before letting anyone talk to them.

Not gonna lie, I respected her for that. It would've been nice to have someone protect me like that, at any point in my life.

"Unless you don't plan on making me wait," Calian said, studying me.

"I don't plan anything. Personal rule. Plans lead to heartache." I grabbed the door. "Thanks for the stuff, but I've gotta go." I swung it shut, and to my surprise and relief, he didn't try to stop me.

With the door closed between us, I let out a breath I hadn't realized I was holding.

I didn't feel as relieved as I would've hoped, though.

I actually kind of missed the big, smirky dude.

Which had to be the fault of whatever ridiculous magic was thundering through my veins now that I'd come to Vevol, because I refused to miss anyone. That was the kind of shit that led to depression, and anxiety, and other mental crap that I most definitely couldn't afford to have. That kind of thing killed women who'd been through the hell I'd survived.

So I grabbed my new bag and dragged the massive thing over to my door. Mare was the only one awake, so I thought it was probably at least sort of early, though I hadn't seen a clock. The sun was up when I answered the door, though, so maybe most people just preferred to sleep in at the Stronghold. I definitely wasn't against that idea, though I wasn't sure I'd be able to get my mind on the same page. Good sleep was a luxury I hadn't had in a long time.

With the door to my room locked, I felt safe as I started unpacking my bag. That was a huge thing for me, feeling safe, but I didn't want to acknowledge it because acknowledgment always led to shittery.

The first thing in the bag was a set of clothes, which I expected.

What I didn't expect was the style of them.

The other girls had clothing that was either from Earth or styled after what we had on Earth. They even had their own styles. Mare had oversized sweatshirts and leggings, North had tight black clothes that covered almost every inch of her, Sunny had old band t-shirts...

Earth clothes.

The things in my bag were definitely not from Earth.

There were multiple pairs of short, thick shorts that reminded me of the shit the preppy volleyball chicks at my high school used to wear, and tank tops made of the same material. The damn thing would leave at least an inch or two of my abdomen on display, and I wasn't even tall. Only average height.

"You have got to be kidding me," I muttered, tossing the clothes onto the bed and grabbing the next pair.

Another pair of booty shorts and another tank top.

Beneath it was more of the same shit.

"Asshole," I snarled, tossing them to the bed.

There was no underwear to go with the clothing, and no bras either.

"You okay in there?" Mare called from the hallway.

My first instinct was to pull back, to keep quiet, but... I actually liked her.

So I crossed the room and opened the door, tossing a hand toward the bed. "That asshole gave me a bag full of lingerie instead of clothes.

Her eyes widened. "Are you serious?"

"Look." I stalked back across the room and plucked one of the sets off the bed, lifting it for her to look at.

Mare relaxed slightly. "I totally get what you're coming from, and it's shitty, but the fae don't consider that lingerie. They gave Dots a set of those too, and the fae who brought it explained that most phoenixes wear those. She's a phoenix, like you. The constant shifting means that they're constantly catching on fire, and those clothes are both fireproof and stretchy enough to survive shifting. May I?" She held a hand out toward me, and I tossed her the pair.

She pulled on them a bit, showing me how they stretched. "Supposedly, these outfits are extremely expensive, which is why Dots only got one. If Lian brought you a couple of pairs, he must've spent his own money on them. The phoenix and hellhound guys are always wearing them, either the shorter or longer version, but most of them only have one or two pairs."

I glanced back down at the pile.

One, two, three, four...

Shit, there were fifteen.

I didn't even have fifteen pairs of clothes back on Earth. I had eight, so I could wash all my shit in one trip to the laundromat, one day a week.

Why the hell would I need fifteen sets of their fancy lingerie?

Maybe lingerie wasn't the right word, if the clothes were only made small because the fabric was expensive...

"How often do they shift, though? I thought you guys never shift?" I asked.

Her expression grew sheepish. "The fae have offered to teach us, but Ana was worried if we spent that much time with any of them, we'd start to like them."

I snorted. "Good old Ana."

"Right?" She laughed, a bit self-consciously. "Supposedly, there's a school that fae created for humans to go to in order to learn how to shift without getting stuck in one form or another. Blood Academy. But it's in the unseelie land, and we belong to the seelies until the five years have passed. Ana will be at Blood Academy right now; that's where the unseelies take us. They're the rule-followers, from what we know, so even Ana wasn't nervous about that part."

Nope, I did not like that. Belonging to unseelies? Hard pass.

I must've made a face that said how much I didn't like that idea.

"It's more like they've got first dibs," Dots said, stepping into the doorway and leaning heavily against the wall. Her golden hair was wrecked, and there were a few spots of what had to be drool on the collar of the gigantic t-shirt she had on, with no pants beneath it or anything. "One of the guys told me that the seelies are the ones who figured out how to break into Earth on the Winter Solstice about twenty years ago, so they made the five-year rule to buy themselves time to convince us to fall in love with them. It's been an epic failure though; only two seelie guys have ever found their mates. And both women convinced the men to join the unseelie, afterward. So there are fifteen previously-human chicks in the unseelie court, and only five of us here."

Shit.

That was probably why the unseelie guy had been so interested in Calian's new obsession with me.

"Have any of you guys shifted before?" I asked.

"Nah. We can all feel the discomfort of the wild magic beneath our skin, trying to break out, but we're professionals at ignoring it at this point." Mare winked at me. "I don't think Calian sees that in your future, though."

My gaze lowered back to the pile of expensive clothes.

"Those are actually way more comfortable than they look. I wear mine as underwear. Haven't worn actual panties or bras in the two years I've been here." She lifted the hem off her huge t-shirt, and my eyebrows shot up when I saw the short-shorts and tank top she had on. There was no way she could've known we were talking about those outfits, which meant she genuinely liked to wear them.

"Seriously, she washes them every day. It's kind of disgusting," Mare teased.

Despite their jokes, I was looking at the clothing items with a lot less anger now.

"So, he was being thoughtful," I finally, reluctantly said.

"Mmhm," Mare agreed.

"And from what I understand, now that you've found your mate, your magic will grow more uncontrollable, so you'll probably start shifting soon," Dots added.

Damn, I wasn't looking forward to that.

Although, phoenixes were massive birds... so could they fly?

It was probably my luck to be a damned flaming flamingo, with wings that didn't even work, so I wasn't going let myself get hopeful about that.

"Ladies!" Sunny yelled from the living area. "You're going to want to see this!"

I exchanged confused glances with Dots and Mare before we all headed out of my room—but I did stop long enough to close the door behind me. Just in case.

One of the bookshelves against the wall had been stripped and dragged to the side, and the couches next to it were loaded with books. A large window was built into the wall, but had been completely hidden by the bookshelf the day before.

Through the window, I could see that a fight was going on. I couldn't see who was fighting, but I saw flying fists, heaving bare chests, thick arms, and insanely-large thighs. There were a few people—well, a few fae—beating the shit out of each other.

"I didn't know there were windows," I said, my eyes glued to the fight.

"Ana hid them all behind bookshelves," Mare murmured, her eyes just as glued to the fight as mine were.

"I'm out." Dots beelined it for her room.

I looked in her direction, frowning as her door shut hard.

"Abusive dad growing up. Abusive boyfriend from sixteen to twenty-two. Life's been a lot better for her since she accidentally got transported here," Sunny told me. "And she wouldn't mind me telling you. We're a family, for better or worse."

Damn.

That made my throat close up, just a little.

One of the guys slammed his fist into another's face, knocking him out.

I winced at the sight—and then froze when Calian grabbed the next guy.

He was the one who had knocked the other one out.

Oh, shit.

"Is this my fault?" I asked aloud.

"I'm thinking yes..." Mare trailed off.

Another two gigantic guys went down.

Calian was a damn *beast*.

Sunny whistled. "Guess we know why he's sort of their king."

My gaze jerked toward her. "He's *what*?"

"The unseelie don't have packs, or families, or organization at all. The Wild Hunt keeps everyone safe... and Lian runs it, even if the others won't admit it. One of his buddies told me that," Sunny said, her gaze glued to the fight. "The running joke is that he's the Savage King. The unseelie king, who is actually a king, they call the Tamed King. He's a really boring guy but apparently already mated to a previously-human chick."

"Damn."

I continued staring out the window.

The more I saw, the more I understood the word used to describe him.

Savage.

I had seen more fights than most people could imagine, but I'd never seen anyone move like that. So easily, like fighting came as naturally to him as breathing.

The fae guys went down, one, by one, by one.

All of us watched, both in awe and horror.

"These guys believe in soulmates," Mare whispered to me.

"Not the same way we do, though. They think you have multiple possible soulmates, but the bond doesn't grow until you've picked one. Your magic will grow wilder and more uncontrollable until you're bonded, though, after you've met a potential mate. If word spreads that the king started bonding to you..." She trailed off. "Usually, they have five years to meet us for themselves, so they can decide whether or not they want us."

"How long until the magic gets too wild?" I checked.

"A couple of weeks, I think. Maybe a couple of months. We've never seen it, so all we know is what the other seelie guys told us." Sunny shrugged. "And none of them wanted us."

"Not for lack of trying," Mare muttered.

I felt bad, but didn't know what else to say.

The fighting finally ended as the last fae crashed to the ground, leaving Calian standing on his own. He wiped a bit of blood from beneath his nose—it looked like it had been broken—and smeared it on the blood-spattered tank top he had on.

Then he stepped back and leaned up against the window.

The whole stronghold was invisible, somehow, so he probably didn't know it was a window.

I stared at his biceps, though.

So.

Damn.

Huge.

The other fae began to get up. I couldn't hear what they were saying, but they looked angry.

Some of them clenched their fists.

"They're going to start fighting again," Sunny said, surprise flooding her voice.

"I'm not sure whether to sit down and enjoy the show with some kind of sick satisfaction or try to intervene," Mare admitted.

Sunny stepped around the couch closest to us and dropped onto the cushions. "What do you think they're fighting over?"

"The guys probably want to meet January, to see if she's their potential mate too. If I had to guess, I'd say Lian's answer is no, and they don't like it."

My face paled.

Shit, what if that really *was* what they were fighting over?

The fighting had made Dots uncomfortable in her own home, and I knew how shitty that was.

"If they don't stop soon, I'll go out there and break it up," I said, biting my lip and hoping the fight would come to an end.

Another fae went down, and another, and another.

How long would Calian really last with all of those guys coming at him?

EIGHT

THERE WASN'T a clock to let me know how much time passed, but I waited as long as I could stomach it before going out there. I'd seen too many fights, but that didn't mean I enjoyed watching them. And eventually, I got too damn tired of watching Calian pummel people.

Plus, they were tiring him out. He was taking more hits—and his nose was bleeding more—the longer he stayed out there.

Something about that made me feel more nauseous than the way he knocked them out so easily. The fae healed so fast that it wasn't even a big deal to get knocked out, but his blood...

No, I was *not* going to sit around and think about why I hated seeing him bleeding so damn much.

"Good luck," Mare murmured, looking more ill than my twisted abdomen felt.

"May the force be with you," Sunny called, her fingers lifted toward me with the middle and ring finger separated. I was pretty sure the hand thing was something from *Star Trek*, and the *force* thing from *Star Wars*, and bit back a snort at the pop culture references.

I was getting slightly faster at undoing all the locks, but still struggled with some of the heavier ones. A couple minutes had gone by when I finally tugged the heavy-ass door open, and I reeled backward when I found the men fighting right outside the door. There were a lot more of them than I thought there had been when I'd been looking out the window, and—

"Get back inside and lock the damn door," Calian snarled at me, interrupting my thoughts.

His cursing—and his anger—surprised me.

He'd been so *tame* the last few times we talked.

It caught me off guard, but I recovered quickly.

"Why the *hell* are you fighting right outside my house?"

Technically, the Stronghold wasn't mine, or really a house, but I was rolling with it.

"Get back inside."

His voice was rougher, and sharper. If I had been someone softer, maybe the change would've scared me. But I understood anger, and could tell his wasn't directed at me.

"Stop fighting," I snarled back.

Someone's fist collided with his temple, and he staggered backward a bit.

Shit, that was a hard hit. Hard enough to kill a human man, at least.

Enough was enough.

I shoved past a few men, who seemed to be waiting their turns for a fight or something, and threw myself between Calian and the guy hauling ass toward him.

My self-preservation wasn't really shining in that moment, but I had healed really fast the day before.

And I was a phoenix, so according to my knowledge, I may as well have been unkillable.

Multiple men roared as two of the fae barreled toward me.

Time seemed to slow down.

The men's eyes went huge; they couldn't stop.

Adrenaline pounded in my chest, loud enough to flood my ears with the sound of my heartbeat.

Calian ripped me backward, his back crashing to the dirt loud enough to rattle both of our bones. He rolled us both, twice, before we stopped. In an instant, he was crouched over me, shifting and roaring.

I gawked upward as the gorgeous man morphed into a massive gray dragon.

Some of the fae scattered.

Others shifted too.

And in a few moments, I was flat on my back, staring out at a group of mystical creatures in shock.

There were dragons.

There were phoenixes.

There were basilisks.

There were sabertooth *creatures*.

There were even fiery hellhounds.

Most of them were snarling.

All of them looked furious.

But none looked quite as pissed as the dragon above me, who had literal fire licking off his scales, curling into the air.

Maybe dragons didn't only *breathe* fire in this world.

Something thrummed within me.

Something foreign, and big, and deadly, and...

Alive.

"Oh, shit," I rasped.

And then, I caught fire too.

It was like the thrumming thing inside me had gotten too big to stay contained.

I felt my body change.

It didn't hurt—it actually felt good. Like stretching, but more dramatic.

My muscles and bones settled into their new positions, and I looked down at myself.

My gigantic legs—or claws, or talons, or whatever you called bird legs—looked as if they were made of gold. But the gold didn't look solid, it looked *molten*, like it was moving or flowing, even though I couldn't feel it in motion.

The feathers that met the golden legs were all the colors of a fire, with reds and oranges and golds and blues and whites melding together. Physical flames danced over them, rustling them as the fire swirled.

Damn...

I was gorgeous.

And strong.

Though I wasn't small, and was definitely solid, I could just barely feel the dragon's chest resting against the top of my head. He was breathing hard—and still roaring at the other fae.

I wanted to duck out from underneath him and spread the large wings I could feel tucked against my sides, but we were already in a shitty situation.

Ducking out?

Bad move.

What I needed to do was shift back so I could talk some sense into the bastard who had been fighting so damn many other fae, but I had no idea how to do that.

As if that one simple thought—that I wanted to shift back—was enough, my body began to change again.

The shift back was just as smooth as the first one had been, my body morphing as if it was something I'd been doing my whole life.

I landed on steady legs, staring in shock at my arms, hands, and the rest of my body.

I had shifted.

Into a damn bird.

There were even a couple of golden feathers on the ground, as physical evidence.

The dragon above me shifted in the blink of an eye, and then was a gigantic fae dude roaring at the other men while blocking me from their sight with his massive body.

I was slightly disoriented, but glanced down at myself and realized quickly why he was blocking me.

Oh, wow.

Yep.

Naked.

No wonder he brought me the fireproof lingerie.

"We have a right to meet her," one of the other men snarled back, speaking above the other growling and snapping creatures. "You can't *claim her.*"

"I can and *did.* Touch her and your life will end. Go ahead; test me."

Something told me this was what the whole savage thing was about. Dude had a murderous streak.

That was my cue to get right the hell out of there.

I took one big step backward—only to have Calian spin around, putting his back to all the men who seemed to want him dead, and plaster his bare chest to mine.

Did I have to wonder if he was naked?

No, I did not. There was definitely an overly-large dick pressed up against my abdomen.

And I *really* didn't hate it as much as I should've.

Like, not at all.

Which was a problem of its own, but one that my future self was going to have to deal with.

"What are you doing?" he growled at me.

"You threatened to kill all of them," I whispered back. "Violently."

His eyes flashed to a steely gray that matched his dragon scales. "You are *mine*."

"That's exactly why I'm leaving. Out of here. Now. Should've been ten minutes ago. Why aren't they attacking you?" I was still whispering, and my words and brain were jumping around like popcorn in the microwave.

"You risked your life already. They won't dare put you in danger again."

"I think I should go. Now." I said curtly, though I didn't move.

"On that, we agree." His words were low and growly.

Before I could try to take a few steps, to walk away on my own, his arms were around my back. He pinned me tighter to his chest, then lifted my feet unceremoniously off the ground and hauled me back to the doorway.

Where he proceeded to set me down on my feet.

And then he stepped back, and shut the door.

I stared at the back of the thing like it could answer the many concerning questions running through my mind.

But it couldn't.

"Wow," Sunny remarked.

She was sitting on the floor, having apparently pulled a couch up close enough to see out the door. Mare sat next to her, and I swear they would've been eating popcorn if any was available.

"That was better than a movie theater," she added.

"Are you as confused as I am?" I asked her, looking between both of them. "Did you see everything?"

"Yes to both questions," Mare said.

A loud crashing noise had all three of us jerking our gazes back to the window, where we saw that the men had resumed fighting. Only now, they were fighting in their beast forms. Things looked... more intense.

And bloodier.

"I've got to stop this before someone dies," I told the girls. "How?"

"You've got to put some clothes on," Sunny corrected me. "Going out there naked isn't going to do a damn thing."

She was right.

I needed to stop them, though.

Calian had seemed mostly sane before he was surrounded by guys trying to... what, talk to me? Meet me? Sniff me? He'd already threatened the hell out of them to the point where I didn't think any of them would dare try to touch me.

If it would stop them from killing each other, I'd meet every damned fae and each of their dogs. There was nothing that stuck with a person the way a death did.

Nothing.

Despite all of the insanity, I still shuddered as the face of my foster dad crossed my mind.

"I need to get him away from them," I said aloud. "And alone. Using his name is supposed to call on him. Do either of you know what that means exactly?"

Both girls shook their heads.

"Guess I'm going to find out." I paused. "After I get dressed."

I jogged over to my room, which thankfully wasn't far, and slammed the door shut behind me.

After grabbing the first pair of fireproof clothes I could reach, I tugged the charcoal-colored tank over my head. The straps were spaghetti-style, but felt plenty sturdy as it settled into place. And Dots was right; it did somehow hold my boobs in the way a bra should—only far more comfortably.

The shorts were just as comfortable, and for once, I was glad I had ignored my first instinct.

"I'm not sure how this is supposed to work," I mumbled to myself, feeling incredibly stupid as I looked around the room. "Calian?" I spoke his name, and felt a sort of magical tug in my chest that I couldn't explain. "Calian, I'm... calling on you? Come here, I guess?"

My words weren't very magical, but following them, there was a sort of shimmer in the room. Then there was a gigantic, bloody man surging toward me.

He stopped before we collided, blinking in surprise as he looked at me, and then around the room. His pupils were dilated, and he looked even more wild than he had earlier.

I hated that I found it kind of sexy, and ignored the hell out of *that* feeling.

"I can't believe that worked," I said aloud.

His eyes softened slightly. "You used my full name; of course it worked."

"That's not a thing where I'm from," I reminded him.

"Of course." He ran a hand over his head, making his wild, sweaty hair stick up with blood. It was black, so at least the color hid the dark red fairly well.

"You went crazy," I told him, matter-of-factly.

"Not crazy. I knew exactly what I was doing. When your mind is shifted, things just look different." His eyes closed for a moment.

I waited for him to thank me for stopping him from murdering more people, but he didn't.

"I'm pretty sure you owe me a thank-you," I drawled, putting a hand on my hip.

His eyes opened and narrowed at me. "I'm still going to kill any of them who refuse to back down. You're *mine*."

"I don't think you realize how annoying it is to hear that," I shot back. "I'm not a possession. What if I kept calling you mine and started attacking everything that looked at you?"

His eyes flashed, and he took a step toward me, stopping with his chest only a breath away from mine. He leaned his head down, and I tilted mine back. If I'd gone up on my tiptoes, my forehead would've kissed his chin. His voice was low and smooth when he murmured, "Then I'd be a *very* lucky man."

I scowled. "You are so full of it."

"And you are so damn beautiful."

There was a tense moment of silence before I finally stepped back and shook my head, hard.

Maybe if I kept shaking the damn thing, I'd lose the interest in this damned fae that just kept getting bigger and bigger. He was an enigma, and I hated how much I liked that.

"What do those guys want, exactly?" I asked him curtly.

His eyes narrowed. "To spend enough time with you to establish that you are in fact not theirs. Which I already know."

I scowled back at him. "What if you were them?"

"I knew the moment I caught the scents of the other women that they weren't mine, just as I knew the moment I smelled you that you were. The fact that they're too weak or too oblivious to do the same is not my problem."

What a *bastard*.

I had to admit that I could see his point of view, though. My world was every man for himself, same as this one.

"What would we have to do to prove that to them?" I asked.

"Seal the mating bond."

That sounded like going through with a marriage, which was a hard pass from me.

"Or?" I pressed.

His expression darkened. "Meet them. Which is not an option."

I lifted a hand to my hip. "One of us is going to have to give up here, and it's not me." I gestured between us. "I don't know how you seal a mating bond, and that's not even an option at all. So I need to meet all those bastards."

His eyes went glittery gray again. "Like *hell* you do. All it takes to seal a mating bond is a few promises."

A few promises?

Nope, I was not marrying him. Not a chance in hell.

"What's the worst that could happen if I meet them? One of them might think I smell good?" I demanded.

His fists and jaw clenched.

Shit, the dude was really serious about this possession thing.

Why was that hot?

"*No.*" His voice was hard and flat.

"Seriously, Calian. There's got to be a way for you to accept me going out and talking to those guys." I tossed a hand toward the door out. "The other girls said that it's been *years* since any of the seelies have been attracted to a human. There's no way they're all going to want me when all these other gorgeous chicks are being ignored."

He scoffed. "It has nothing to do with *attraction*. Looking for a mate is about *connection*. It's far better to be alone than to be with the wrong person."

"Exactly, and I'm positive I'm the wrong person for everyone. You included, probably, but it seems a little late to convince you of that."

His scowl deepened. "You're one of us. Seelie. When we look at you, we see fire. Freedom. Refusal to fall in line. For most of us, that will be far more than enough connection."

I tossed a hand in the air. "I don't know what to do with you."

"As I don't know what to do with you," he growled back.

"So what, then? What's the solution? There must be something that would make you willing to walk out there with me. I already have too much death on my conscience; I can *not* take another one."

His eyes darkened. "Fly with me."

I blinked.

Okay, that was not what I was expecting.

"Trusting another with your life is the first step in a mate bond. Fly with me, and I'll let you meet them." He paused, then added in a growl, "Assuming you let me touch you while you meet them. I'll need the contact to stop myself from ripping their throats out."

Well...

That honestly wasn't anywhere near as bad as I thought it was going to be.

I could do that, sure.

But I had to be careful about how I told him that. I already knew Calian well enough to know that he was going to take every inch I gave him.

"I don't know," I grumbled. "You're asking too much, Lian."

I'd never called him by his nickname before, but I thought it was kind of hot, so I was going with it.

And I was a shit liar, but I'd known that for years.

His eyes narrowed further. "Should I add that you'll wear my clothing over yours while you meet them?"

Dammit.

This man was a total bastard, and I hated myself for being *here for it.*

"Fine. I'll fly with you after I meet everyone who's gathered, and you can touch me while I meet them. Not intimately, though." I didn't think that last part was necessary, but I added it just in case.

He grunted an agreement.

I figured that answer was as good as it was going to get.

"All right, let's get this shit over with."

NINE

My gaze was glued to his perfect damned ass as he strode over to my newest bag of clothes. He pulled out a few things I hadn't yet gotten through before tugging out a pair of pants that were clearly his.

I looked at the ceiling, pretending I hadn't been staring at his butt as I drawled, "Putting your own clothing in my bag? Pretty big assumption, buddy."

"I'm a big man," he drawled back.

My eyes tried to drop back to his figure, but I forced them to stay trained on the ceiling.

"And it wasn't an assumption. I knew you'd eventually get curious enough or desperate enough to use my name."

"What the hell does that mean?"

"Your magic will grow wilder the longer we go without sealing the mate bond that's begun growing between us. Mine will, too, but I've had longer to learn it than you have. I can shift and fly out the tension that would grow if you refused to see me; you cannot. The longer we're separated, the more at risk you are of wrestling with your magic until it takes control and forces you to spontaneously shift."

Damn.

"Flying will help. Physical contact of any kind, too."

I couldn't hear him getting dressed, but putting pants on wasn't exactly a loud event.

His hand touched my elbow, and my gaze jerked toward him as that weird electric shock feeling cut through me.

"Why does it feel like that?" I asked him, tugging my elbow away.

"It's the concept of mates. Our magic is meant to complete each other. When yours has to nudge mine, or vice versa, we feel the shock."

"What does that mean, though? Nudge?"

He leaned back against one of the walls, and damn, something about having him in front of me, shirtless and massive and gorgeous... it messed with me. "Your feet were wounded in the forest, after you'd been running; my magic met yours, encouraging it to heal you faster and more effectively. It also helps with hunger, exhaustion, pain, and a few other things."

Shit. "Then how can we be compatible with multiple people?"

"That's only a small possibility. And a connection requires compatible magic, nothing else."

My eyebrows shot upward. "So love doesn't matter."

"*Doesn't matter* is subjective." The man studied me carefully. "My people only started finding mates when we discovered your world, and only a fraction of the women we've brought from your world have proven to be potential mates with any of our people. There are no proven rules for mating; all any of us can do is learn as we go."

He continued, "Among the unseelies, the few mated pairs are not together for love, at least as far as I'm aware. As far as the majority of our people know, a mate bond either happens or doesn't the moment you meet, but those of us functioning as leaders of a sort theorize that it can happen slowly, too. We haven't announced that, though, as the women would likely be bombarded."

Damn, that was *not* what I was expecting him to say.

"So when you call me mate and declare that I'm yours, you're not proposing a romantic relationship? No sex, no kissing, nothing except... touchy, claimy friendship?" I checked.

He remained silent for a moment.

I stared back.

"Shall we get going, as you said?" The bastard gestured toward the door.

"Tell me the truth." I put a hand on my hip.

"The truth?" He lifted an eyebrow.

Bastard was totally avoiding the question, and trying to delay his answer.

"Yes, the truth. If you want to be friends, say that straight-out. If you want to be more, say that. I want to know exactly what I'm getting myself into here." I gestured between us.

"Truthfully, I don't know. I assumed when I first caught your scent that I would be looking for the strength that comes with the bond between us. And then I met you."

"And?" I demanded.

"I find myself feeling urges and desires I didn't know were possible." He continued studying me. "I've never heard of this before. This sex you spoke of. How does it work?"

Oh, no.

Hell no.

I was out.

"Let's go." I grabbed him by the stupidly-attractive arm and dragged him toward the door.

"Your reluctance to speak of it tells me it's something I'll be interested in knowing about," he said, his voice low and sexy.

"Fuck off," I growled back.

"That word translates strangely in my language, you know," he countered. "I've wondered for centuries why the word *connect* is such a popular curse among my people. *Fuck* is only a stronger type of connection, or so the translation magic tells me."

I dragged him through the building, ignoring the stares from Mare and Sunny, as well as the words the man was saying.

None of the women had told me that fae dudes didn't know what sex was.

Did they not know?

I guess none of them had mentioned getting propositioned by fae guys, so...

Shit.

Was I supposed to *tell* him?

What if he attacked me if I did?

A shudder tore through my spine at the thought, at the *memories*.

No, I wasn't going to tell him.

No way in hell could I take that risk.

They had to already know about jerking off, but...

No, I was not thinking about that.

We reached the door, and Calian stopped me with a palm to the stone. "Holding your hand won't be enough," he warned me, his voice low. "The level of possessiveness I feel is..." He seemed to search for a word.

"It's fine, I've seen it. This is my part of the bargain, so I'll uphold it. Don't worry." My voice came out softer than I expected it to, but I didn't want to think about that.

He dipped his head in a nod and worked on the top locks while I started from the bottom. He did a couple more than me, but didn't seem to mind that as he stepped back to let me tug the door open.

Of course, when I pulled the thing open, his hand wrapped around my bicep.

He was trying not to just *grab* me, I could tell. But if he was new to boobs, vaginas, and all other things womanly, then he probably wasn't even sure *how* to grab me.

I found myself pulling his hand off my bicep and dragging it down to my hip. He stilled behind me as I turned my back to his chest, and froze in place when I stepped back far enough that my ass met his crotch.

His erection pressed against my butt, thicker and harder than I knew was possible.

I tried to ignore it, and my screaming conscience as I grabbed his other hand and put it on my other hip.

"If your hands are on me, they're not ripping anyone apart," I told him in a low voice.

He didn't respond.

If that was his first time touching a woman, and he'd really been alive for centuries, I didn't blame the guy for being speechless. First times were a weird, unique thing for everyone.

Even ancient fae bastards.

Our bodies remained practically glued together as we stepped through the doorway.

My heart pounded a hell of a lot faster than it should've, and not because we were stepping out into a lion's den—because of the gigantic rock digging into my ass, and the massive hands on my hips. Those damned palms were so big, and my shorts were so short, that he could've dragged his fingers over my bare thighs if he'd tried.

Luckily, he didn't try.

Or unluckily. I guess it probably depended on your perspective.

But that thick strip of his six-pack pressing against my back made me consider another perspective.

A newer, riskier one.

I wouldn't let myself think about it, though.

"This female is mine," Calian told the group, his voice low and certain. "She wishes to let you smell our combined scent, so you can realize she's not yours. Form a line."

The other men didn't move smoothly, or follow any sort of rhythm, but they made their way into a haphazard line that stretched toward us.

Calian held me securely in place against his chest as the first man stepped up to us. His grip on me tightened as the other man leaned in. The man's nostrils flared as he inhaled.

A moment passed, and then he stepped back, turned, and strode back into the forest I'd hiked through.

Calian's grip tightened when the next man stepped forward and repeated the movements of the first. It tightened again with the third man, and again with the fourth.

He was holding me like I was his anchor as the line of fae dudes kept moving. His grip on me was so tight it borderlined on painful, but I loved it.

I *really* loved it.

I'd never had anyone hold me like that before. Like I mattered to them. Like if anyone made a wrong move toward me, they'd find the end of their lives in the hands that held me so fiercely.

It unnerved the hell out of me too, though.

When the crowd finally dispersed, I eased myself away from Calian. He was reluctant, but let me go without a complaint.

The distance I put between us when I took a couple of steps away helped me breathe a lot easier.

"Now, we fly," Calian told me, his gaze intense as he stared at me.

I jerked my head in a nod, looking at the forest and focusing my attention out there.

I just wanted...

Well, I didn't know what I wanted.

But I had promised a flight, so that's what I was going to do.

My gaze followed Calian's hands to the waistband of his pants, and tracked them as he stripped the clothing off.

Holy hell.

The man was ginormous.

I tried not to stare at his monstrous dick, but totally failed.

When he started changing forms, his intense gaze burning into my damn soul, my gaze followed him.

Something about the way his body morphed and grew and changed was sort of beautiful.

The curve of his huge, smooth head.

The glittering expanse of his wings.

The stretch of his neck as he raised it, his chin lifting.

He was preening for me, I realized, and barely bit back a grin.

This whole damned world was something else altogether.

"I haven't really seen any other dragons," I remarked, stepping up closer to him. His body tensed as I reached a hand toward his body, and I looked up at him, frowning.

His head turned and lowered toward me, giving me permission to touch him, so I carefully lifted it and pressed it to his scales.

They were insanely smooth, and much warmer than I expected.

"You're amazing," I admitted to him, slowly moving my hand over his head. His eyes closed, and he blew a puff of hot air toward me.

A laugh escaped me, and I pulled my hand away.

He stepped back just a little, and then lowered himself to the ground. His head dropped to the dirt, and he gave me an expectant look.

Another laugh almost escaped me.

He was kind of adorable.

Not that I was into adorable—or him.

I wasn't sure how to climb onto a dragon, so I eyed him.

He puffed a little smoke toward me and then wiggled closer.

Fighting another grin, I reached an arm up to his gigantic neck and tried to throw a leg upward. When I moved, he rolled sideways to meet me.

A slightly-terrifying moment later, I was settled on his back with my face snuggled up against his warm, smooth neck.

The thrill of it had my chest clenching, my heartbeat thudding loudly. That magic inside me seemed to be thrumming faster, like it had been earlier when I shifted.

Calian tilted his head back, stretching his neck out and letting loose a thick jet of fire.

Gray flames danced down his neck, reaching toward me.

Despite my instinct to move away from them, to slide off of him or find a way down, I reached toward him.

I had erupted into flames myself earlier, so no matter what my instincts said, his fire wasn't going to kill me.

Calian took off from the ground as his flames circled my wrists, flooding me with a strange, magical heat. The wind whipped against my face, my hair, and my arms, but I didn't pay it a shred of mind; the magic had me completely and utterly enthralled.

Lian's fire snaked its way to my shoulder and then over my torso, growing thicker and brighter as it continued to climb over my body.

The world around me flickered whitish blue, and a heady electric charge cut through my body.

My eyes closed, and everything seemed to spin for a moment.

The heat and flames began to die down, then.

The spinning around me seemed to slow, and I found myself relaxing. My hand on Calian's scales still felt hot, but it also felt right. There was a calmness that accompanied the physical contact, one that I didn't have a name for.

It almost felt like safety.

Whatever it was, a girl could get addicted to a feeling like that.

I found myself leaning down against his neck, my cheek pressed to his scales as my eyes traced the world below us. The forest was so vibrant and alive, the clouds puffy and swirling in the thick wind blowing past us. It didn't seem to mind that Calian was creating his own wind; it just kept moving.

The dragon glanced back at me, as if to reassure himself that I was still there and alive, before he soared higher. My heart and magic thrummed within me, and I felt the power growing wilder, the way he'd told me it would if we didn't seal our bond. It twisted within me, swelling and arching, until I was struggling to breathe.

His voice pierced my mind, a soft but firm stab toward some invisible, undefinable part of me. *"Fly with me, mate."*

As if that was the only encouragement it needed, my magic burst into life.

I felt myself slide off Calian's back as the shift happened. For one heart-wrenching moment, I was free-falling.

Then my wings were spread in the wind, and I was no longer falling.

I was flying.

My heart still pounded, and my head still spun, but now the feelings crowding my mind were ones I'd never known.

Freedom.

Joy.

Peace.

Bliss.

Hope.

The emotions were so strong and thick that my throat was swollen, even in its strange new form.

I had thrown that coin into the fountain and asked the world for a way out, and it had given me something even better.

A second chance at life.

Not just any life, either—a happy life.

If I would've been human in that moment, the eyes that I'd spent so many years training not to cry would've been watering.

I didn't have to fight just to survive anymore.

If I wanted to, now, I could live.

Love.

Enjoy.

My instincts screamed at me that it was just a dream. That the first moment I let myself feel this hope, I would lose everything once again and find myself even worse off than I'd been before.

But for once, I ignored those instincts.

And as fire licked the feathers on my new, powerful body, I let myself love my life so much it hurt.

TEN

TIME FLEW past as Calian and I soared over the forest. I knew which direction I would need to fly to get back to the Stronghold, even though I wasn't sure I could find the clearing easily, and that made me feel better.

When we finally landed, the sun was setting behind the forest. I was grinning like a crazy person, my heartbeat even and happy just like the rest of me.

I had never felt that good before. Not for one minute of my life on Earth.

Calian shifted faster than I did. His nudity didn't faze me as I lunged toward him, throwing myself at him. My arms wrapped around his neck as I hugged his body fiercely to mine, gratitude thick enough to drown a dolphin making my throat swell again.

"That was amazing," I told Calian, squeezing him tightly.

"It was," he murmured, his arms wrapping around my back until his grip on me was as tight as mine on him.

"Thank you," I whispered, my damned eyes stinging. "Thank you so much."

"You shouldn't thank me for something that brought me pleasure, January."

"Just Ari. But shut up and let me thank you."

He chuckled, the sound low and sexy.

I was too exhausted and exhilarated to care. There was a bit of an electric current running between us, too, but I barely noticed it as it slowly worked to drain my exhaustion away.

"Fly with me again tomorrow?" he murmured, his hands sliding up my back until one of them cradled my neck.

I jerked my head in a nod. "Definitely."

"There will be more men outside come morning. I can feel their energy now as they watch us."

The back of my neck prickled, and I fought the urge to turn and look around. "Don't kill them while I sleep," I whispered.

He gave me another low chuckle. "I make no promises."

I bit my lip. "Seriously?"

"If any of them have decided your scent calls to them, they'll try to kill me for the chance to pursue you. So yes, seriously."

Damn him.

"Can you just... sleep on the floor of my room or something? That wouldn't be breaking any rules, right?" I checked.

"There are no rules," he said, his voice flooded with humor and something else I didn't have a name for. "And yes, if you wish, I can sleep in your room."

Good.

No one would die, then.

And since he didn't know about sex, I wouldn't have to worry about him pulling any sketchy shit.

"Okay, then... come on." I stepped back, slipping my hand into his. I tried not to let our fingers slide between each other, but failed, and the damn things knitted together like they had minds of their own.

I kept walking, towing him with me.

We knocked on the door and waited for one of the other girls to open it. Sunny finally answered wearing a big ole' smirk.

"Don't," I warned her, stepping past and tugging Calian in behind me.

"Mmhmm," she said, so damn much sass in that one sound.

I tried to pull my hand out of his, but he picked that moment to tighten his grip, like he'd been expecting me to pull that shit.

I led Calian into my room behind me, and shut the door hard.

He stopped a short way into the room, studying me again as I stood with my back to the door. "You like them."

I knew he was talking about the other women, and I didn't want to acknowledge it. "I don't like much of anything."

His gaze grew a bit curious. "There must be things you liked about Earth."

"If there were, I wouldn't have wished to get away from it."

Suddenly questioning my decision to bring the man into my bedroom, I stepped past him and padded across the room. "I'm going to shower. Stay out here." I'd lock the door, but the warning would help.

After grabbing another pair of the clothes I'd left strewn all over my bed like a damned slob, I ducked into the room and shut the door.

Having the slab of stone between me and Calian made me feel slightly better, even if I knew he could probably break through it if he wanted.

I rested my back against it, my eyes closing.

There was a quick knock on the door a moment later. "January?" Lian murmured.

It didn't seem to matter how many times I told him to call me Ari.

"What?"

"Would you mind if I stepped out to make you something to eat? Or would you rather I wait until you're finished in the shower?"

My mind blanked for a long moment.

Had he just... asked me what I wanted?

What the hell?

Who did that?

"Uh..." I paused after saying the word, not sure what I would prefer.

I definitely wouldn't say no to food, but something about the idea of him being out there chatting with the other human girls while I was in the shower made my jaw clench.

"Just wait for me," I finally said.

"Of course." His voice was soft, but I could picture that damned gorgeous smirk of his.

I stepped further into the bathroom, and my gaze caught on my reflection in the mirror.

Damn, I looked... different.

My hair was still its usual dark blonde, but the color seemed richer. Shinier.

When I turned my head, I noticed that my ears were pointed at the edges and lifted my fingers up to them, to trace the new shape.

"Damn," I murmured to myself.

Physically, my body shape was the same—curvy, but not super curvy—only my skin looked sort of... glowy.

When I got closer to the mirror to see my eyes better, I was startled to see that their usual muddy brown had morphed into a vibrant green color that reminded me of the leaves on so many of those crazy-looking trees in the forest.

My gaze traced my arms and legs, looking for some kind of magical tattoo. Disappointment flooded me when all I found was more glowy skin.

Oh well, I'd survive.

Glancing over at the shower, I hesitated. I'd been on fire for most of the day—literally—and didn't feel dirty in the slightest. I actually felt really, really good.

And food sounded great, even though I wasn't very hungry.

Would it be gross to forgo a shower in favor of watching the fae dude who claimed I was his cook for me?

I guessed I could help him, too, if I wanted to be nice.

My teeth caught on my bottom lip while I debated my options.

Ultimately, the smartest choice would've been to take a long shower and then feign exhaustion and go to sleep. That would buy me time away from Calian and the other girls, and prevent me from bonding with them further in any way that might make me sad when they inevitably ended up treating me shitty, betraying me, or being taken away.

My self-preservation instincts had my thoughts spiraling into defense mode, preparing for the worst.

But the hope and happiness that had begun to sprout in my chest while I was flying whispered that I should make another choice.

One that I would *enjoy*.

I didn't want to accept that I was choosing hope, but I found myself yanking the door open anyway. My eyes widened when I found Calian putting the clothes I'd left on the bed away in the closet.

He glanced over his shoulder at me, and my chest squeezed when he gave me a slow, sexy smile.

Panic had me shutting the door again, harder.

Nope.

Screw off, hope.

Shower it was.

ELEVEN

HALF AN HOUR LATER, I padded out of the bathroom, wrapped in a towel. My body was so relaxed from all the warm water that I couldn't even bring myself to worry about the man I knew would be somewhere in the room, waiting for me.

And yep, there he was: sprawled across my bed like he owned the damn thing.

He was the one who had picked up the blankets and sheet and everything else from wherever it had been before he gave it to me, so I couldn't exactly hold it against him. Plus, he looked really damn delicious draped over the bed like that, which did a number on whatever anger I should've felt.

My hair hung tangled down my back, water dripping from the ends as I headed to the closet. The bags and everything that had been inside them were put away, and as expected, I found them tucked neatly into the closet along with the rest of my clothes. My gaze dragged over all the pairs of comfortable, fireproof clothing, but lingered the longest on the section that I hadn't seen yet.

A few pairs of pants (way too long to be my own) and a couple of muscle-tees like the one Calian had been wearing the day we met.

So I could wear my clothes... or his.

So many options.

I didn't mind that fact as much as I expected to.

The shorts and tank top felt like another layer of skin as I pulled them on. Most of them were in shades of black and gray, which I liked, but I picked out a set that was made of deep crimson fabric. Something about the color reminded me of flying, and I loved flying.

I didn't want to go out and hang with the girls in shorts that only covered a little more than underwear, so I grabbed a pair of Calian's pants and tugged them up my legs. The fabric was thin and ridiculously soft, and I found myself petting it like it was a damn dog.

That was weird, I knew, so I stopped before I stepped out of the closet.

His eyes devoured me the moment he could see me again, the orbs hooded as he just *stared*.

How was he so damned gorgeous?

And how did he make me feel so much, especially when I was trying so hard not to be affected by him?

"Ready?" he asked.

"Yep." I tried not to let him see how much he was affecting me. "Let's go."

The man eased himself up off the mattress, and I almost drooled at the way his abs looked while he moved.

He grabbed one of his tees off the dresser and tugged it on before he pulled the door open. When he gestured for me to go first, I slid through, ignoring the way his eyes made me feel like my damned skin was burning.

"You're beautiful," he murmured to me.

I ignored the compliment, but felt my face flushing anyway.

"The kitchen's over here," I told him, feeling a couple of stares on us as we walked. Sunny, Mare, and Dots were on the couch, watching a movie, as far as I could tell without looking back at him.

"She'd better be tapping that," Sunny muttered.

"I'd give up a boob," Dots agreed.

My face flushed hotter.

This was a terrible idea.

"Maybe we should—" I began, but Calian cut me off by grabbing me by the waist. He set me on the countertop in one fluid motion, not at all winded by having just dead-lifted my heavy ass.

"You don't know our spices, I assume," he said, brushing a chunk of wet hair off my face with the back of his fingers. I acted like the touch hadn't made goosebumps erupt over my arms and legs.

"I don't know any of your foods," I agreed. "The main thing we eat here seems like your version of our rice and beans, but tastes better."

He made a noncommittal noise. "No one taught you how to make it."

I looked at the other girls. They were the ones who had cooked.

Mare shook her head, though she was fighting a smile.

"They figured it out," I told Calian, looking back at him.

He flashed me a smirk. "I'm sure they did."

The man turned back to the stove. He didn't move flawlessly through the human-style kitchen, but also didn't have a problem going through cupboards to find everything he needed. I found myself studying every movement he made, tracking his body and following every move of his muscles.

He didn't touch my hair again as he cooked, but explained to me the names of each of the foods, as well as what kind of plant they came from. It turned out that the "beans" we'd been eating were meant to be boiled, mashed, and then whipped, and the "rice" was supposed to be fried in a pan with a bit of some strange kind of oil.

When he started seasoning things, he filled a tiny bowl with the oil and dipped a finger into it, before shaking a tiny bit of the seasoning onto his finger and holding it out to me. "Taste."

I stared at him for a long moment before finally shaking my head and forcing myself to snap out of it. "What?"

"Taste, so you know the flavor." His lips were curved up in a wicked smirk. "Unless you're scared."

Bastard.

He must've already realized that I typically refused to admit to being or feeling scared. Fear was good for nothing other than realizing that shit was about to hit the damned fan.

"So much better than a movie," Dots whispered from the living room.

I flipped her the bird without looking over, and earned a round of snorts and quiet laughs.

Bitches.

I hated that I liked them.

With a sigh, I parted my lips.

He slipped his finger into my mouth, and left it there as I licked the seasoning off the huge digit.

The flavors that hit my tongue were nothing I had words to describe—but tasted really good.

"Wow," I managed, as he pulled his finger away and put it in his own mouth.

Nope, I was not acknowledging that he'd licked my saliva off his skin.

He washed his hands with the bar of rough soap beside the sink, then returned to cooking.

I thought I was in the clear, but after a couple of minutes passed, he repeated the process with another spice.

His smirk was back, his gaze hot as he lifted his finger to my lips.

*Ooh*s and snorts came from the peanut gallery again, and I ignored them this time.

"I can do it myself," I countered, pushing his hand away.

His eyes turned the gray of his dragon form, and he reached forward, dragging his finger over my bottom lip. The touch surprised me, and the warmth that slowly blossomed on my skin was weird.

My tongue slid out to drag over the seasoning, surprising me with its light, sweet flavor.

"This one is rubbed into the skin when someone is sore or in pain," he told me, lifting his finger back to his lips and cleaning it quickly. "It warms and relaxes you. Makes injuries bearable."

"What would happen if someone put it on their genitals?" one of the girls asked from the other room.

Dammit, Dots.

"Theoretically," she added hastily.

Calian didn't so much as glance at her, his intense gaze focused solely on me. "Hours of fierce pleasure." His eyes lowered to my lips. The bottom one was still warm and tingly, and starting to feeling a bit swollen too, but not in an uncomfortable way.

"Get back to cooking," I grumbled at the man.

A smirk teased his lips again, his body relaxing as he turned back to the stove.

My mind spun a bit.

He didn't know about sex... but of course, he knew about masturbating. There was no way that, in a world full of men, no one had figured out how to jack off.

Dammit. Now I had that oh-so-pleasant thought keeping me company.

He repeated the tasting thing a few more times as he made our meal. Despite the intensity of the last thing he made me taste, I parted my lips when he brought his finger to them.

I was weak...

And he was gorgeous.

And the fact that he was giving me his complete attention while also cooking for me did not pass my notice.

. . .

CALIAN'S VERSION of beans and rice was a hell of a lot better than ours. The rest of the girls and I downed it like we were starving, all of us seated randomly around the couch, and North in her room of course. Mare had been writing notes while Lian was cooking, and she questioned him further while we ate. He was relaxed, sitting a little too close to me and working on his own bowl of food.

When we were done, the girls turned the movie they had been watching back on. It was a chick flick, which I wasn't sure I really wanted Calian to see, but I didn't want to take him back to my room either.

We watched for about an hour before things got steamy—and my face got really damn red.

Calian was watching the screen with way too much interest, so I grabbed his hand and towed him to my bedroom, muttering a goodnight.

The bastard was going to have way too many questions for me.

He didn't ask a thing though, as I locked the door and made my way over to the bed. When I plopped down on it, I sprawled out over the middle so the bastard would know I wasn't inviting him to sleep with me.

The room was dead silent after he settled on the ground, a couple feet away from my bed.

I felt like a total bitch for not giving him a blanket or pillow, but I only had one of each.

A few long, long minutes passed before I got too stressed to leave the silence between us. "Well?" I demanded.

"Well what?" He sounded amused.

"You must have questions."

"You don't seem interested in answering them, so I planned to keep them to myself." His voice was soft and playful, and I hated the way it calmed my anxiety so immediately.

A heavy sigh escaped me.

I couldn't believe I was going to do it, but...

I was going to do it.

"You've gathered that women's bodies are built differently than men's. You have dicks."

"And you do not," he agreed, his voice still playful.

I grimaced up at the ceiling. "We have breasts and vaginas, instead. Which you've seen. Or at least felt, when we were naked together. Vaginas are... weird."

He was quiet, giving me more time to explain.

"They're sort of the opposite of dicks. Dicks stick out, and vag's... go in. It's kind of like a body-cave. Which sounds disgusting, and is, but dudes like them. Sex is when a dick goes inside a vagina. It's a tight fit, but it works. Theoretically, it's supposed to be pleasurable for both people, but most of the time it's only good for the guy."

The moment was long, tense, and awkward, but there was no way around it. He had to know. And at least he could tell his fae buddies himself, so no other human chicks would have to have the same weird conversation with other dudes.

"That's not a secret," I added. "'You should tell the other guys, so it's not so awkward."

More silence ensued.

Too much silence.

"Are you good?" I asked him.

"If extremely hard and vivaciously curious translates to *good* in your language, then yes," he murmured.

A snort escaped me, and a low laugh came from his side of the room.

A few moments passed before Calian spoke again. "I can understand how sex would be pleasurable for a man, but how does a woman's pleasure work?"

Oh.

Awkward.

Might as well get it over with.

"It's weird. Women have a thing on the outside of their vagina called a clit. It's kind of like a pleasure button, if you use it right. There's another pleasure point inside of a vagina called a g-spot, too, but they're pretty much impossible for guys to find. There are a ton of jokes about them back on Earth because of how shitty men are at making them work.

"Mmm." Calian's voice was low, but flooded with interest. "I assume you've never had a man find yours."

"You assume correctly." I stared at the ceiling, my humor fading. "There's another thing back on Earth, we call it sexual assault. Or rape. It's when a guy forces himself on a woman. You don't have anything like that here, right? Between men or women?"

He growled, "Of course we don't. We like killing far too much. If anyone so much as considered something like that, their death would be horrible."

That made me feel slightly better, even though liking killing didn't exactly seem like a logical reason to not have sexual assault.

"Did that happen to you on Earth?" Calian asked me a few minutes later, his voice lower and deadlier.

I bit my lip, but didn't answer.

"Should any man give you any unwanted touch in my world, you tell me immediately. I will relish his dismemberment," the fae told me.

My throat swelled, but I said nothing.

"Should I ever do anything to hurt you, there's a chink in every dragon's scales. A soft, vulnerable spot, where a knife will end his life instantly. It's in a different place on every dragon, and mine is on the inside of my left thigh, regardless of my form."

Regardless of his form?

"I don't know what that means," I whispered back, though I did know.

He was giving me a way to kill him, in case he ever hurt me.

"Come here," he told me, his voice quiet.

I didn't get up at first, but then curiosity and trust engulfed me so thickly that I could no longer ignore them.

My feet landed on the cold stone, and I shivered a little as I crossed the room. When I kneeled beside Calian, he was already sprawled out on the floor, no pillow or blanket in sight just like I expected.

"Can I take your fingers to the spot?" he asked me, his voice low and steady. His eyes were so gorgeous, the damn things practically held me captive.

I jerked my head in a nod, putting my hand to his.

He dragged my hand over his thigh, and neither of us acknowledged the erection bulging so obviously in the soft material of his pants.

"It's a depression in my skin," he murmured, his fingers wrapping around mine until he had my pointer finger out. When he pressed it lightly into a spot inside his thigh, I felt a small indentation. It was smaller than my pinky, but when I pressed carefully against it, I felt that the skin in that spot was much, much softer than the area around it.

"Can I feel without clothes?" I asked him.

Maybe it was stupid, or ridiculous, but I wanted to know exactly where his weak spot was. Not because I expected I'd need to kill him, but... because I just wanted to know, I supposed.

"You don't need permission, mate. I'm yours to touch," he said, releasing my hand.

I guessed he wasn't going to guide my hand if I put it in his pants, but I didn't mind that.

The fingers touching the spot through his clothes remained where they were, and my other hand slid under the waistband of his pants.

His whole body tensed as my palm dragged over his bare pelvis, past the erection that bobbed for me as I moved past it. His eyes closed, and his jaw clenched as he leaned his head back.

"Are you okay?" I whispered to him, as my fingers found the spot.

He made an agreement-like noise, his jaw still clenched.

My thumb dragged over the *chink in his scales*, and my bare arm brushed against the side of his erection.

We both froze for a moment.

His cock bobbed against the side of my arm, the hot, hard silk dragging against me.

"Shit," I finally whispered. "Sorry."

I carefully withdrew my arm from his pants, trying not to drag it over his erection.

"Do human women often apologize for giving a man the most pleasure he's experienced in his entire life?" Calian asked me, his voice gravelly.

My face flushed. "No."

"Then withdraw yours, January."

I bit my lip. "How does one withdraw an apology?"

"Usually a simple, 'never mind, I'm not sorry,' suffices," Calian drawled back.

His cock was still bobbing in those damn soft pants, though, and the thing was practically hypnotizing me.

I bit my lip harder.

Was I sorry for feeling him?

No, I was not.

And I wasn't about to give him a damned handjob, but *withdrawing an apology* seemed so pointless.

"On Earth, we don't withdraw apologies. We just do things to cancel them out. Like..." I slid my hand into his pants again and wrapped my fingers around the top of his cock, squeezing him. He was so freaking huge, and I could feel a bit of his hot desire leaking on my hand from the head of him. "See? Not sorry."

"Not sorry indeed." His voice was strained.

I couldn't help it; I pumped my hand down his length once, and then dragged it back up.

A snarl escaped him, and he grabbed his erection around my fist as it throbbed with his pleasure, soaking both my fist and his pants.

Shocked pride cut through me, and my body flushed something fierce.

"I am so sorry," he growled at me. "I—"

"No, don't be. I feel... sexy." An awkward laugh escaped me. "And powerful. That's kind of a rush, huh?"

His eyes pierced me to the damn soul, and he said nothing.

I slowly slipped my hand out of his pants, then stood and went into the bathroom.

His eyes tracked me the whole way.

Soap lathered over my fingers as I scrubbed them clean, my mind spinning.

I'd never been completely relaxed with a man since I was attacked. I'd had sex a few times, just to prove to myself that I could, but I'd always felt like he had the power. Like if he wanted to, he could hurt me. And that had scared the hell out of me.

But back there, with Calian, I had felt strong. Powerful.

All I'd done was touch him, and he'd erupted all over my hand.

I had done that; made him feel good.

And shit, that made me feel like I was in charge.

What if *sex* could feel like that?

What if he could get me off, too, and I could feel like that while he did?

What if I could actually enjoy myself while he was touching me, and lose it the way he had?

Did I want that?

My heart clenched.

I did.

I really, really did.

The connection, the relaxation, the pleasure...

It was thrilling.

I couldn't just go out and ask him to touch me though, could I? He hadn't even known what a vagina was, and he wasn't expecting us to fall in love despite our mate-connection thing.

But if he wasn't expecting love...

Well, then maybe the bond between us was perfect.

I could call the shots.

We could make each other feel good.

And the connection between us was so strong and permanent that even if we didn't fall in love, it wouldn't matter. We could just be friends who had awesome sex.

Shit, that sounded amazing.

My mind was made up, as I slipped back out of the bathroom.

We were going to be friends with benefits.

TWELVE

CALIAN HAD CHANGED into a pair of clean pants and was sitting on the edge of the mattress, shirtless, when I walked back into the room. His arms were positioned on the bed behind him, his body sprawled out, somehow both relaxed and tensed at the same time.

Damn, what a masterpiece.

His eyes tracked my movement like I was his prey.

I'd left my pants in the bathroom, so my legs were mostly bare.

His gaze stroked my skin. Though the room was dark, I felt like he could see every inch of me.

"Thank you," he said to me, his voice low and sensual.

"On Earth, we *show* our thanks." I sat down on his lap, and noticed his fingers dig into the blanket.

"I didn't know if that would be welcome." His eyes dragged over my face and then down to the swell of my breasts, where they lingered. "Nor do I have the experience you deserve from a man who would touch you."

"Not all women want man-whores," I countered.

He gave a low chuckle. "Do I want to know what that means?"

"Probably not." I eased myself further up his thighs, so his erection pressed exactly where I wanted it, but didn't rock against him. The pressure was light, making my body throb. "You don't know what you're doing—but I know exactly how I want you to touch me, and I'm pretty damn sure you're willing to figure it out."

"More than you know." He leaned upward, changing the angle he pressed into me, and my body tensed.

"Put your hands on my hips," I told him, rocking against him lightly. "Touch me however you want."

His hands lifted to my waist, skipping my hips because they were covered. His fingers dragged slowly and reverently over the bare skin there, stroking and tracing it while I continued moving against him, just enough to make myself even more horny.

His hands slid under the hem of my tank, the thick digits dragging over my ribcage.

"Tell me what you're thinking," I told to him, trying not to arch too much as he moved toward my breasts.

"I want to bury my face between your thighs and inhale your scent." His voice was low, his hands sliding further up my ribs until his fingertips found the undersides of my breasts.

I hadn't realized the undersides were sensitive, but when he touched them like that, they sure as hell were.

He took his sweet time, stroking them slowly, taking in every inch of my skin as his hands moved upward. When they finally found my nipples, my head dropped backward and I pressed closer to him, fighting a moan.

"I want to feel these hard tips on my tongue," he said, his voice lower and more gravelly. "I want you to lose yourself to pleasure while I devour your breasts with my hands, with my tongue, with my teeth."

When I started to open my mouth, to tell him that orgasming from tit play alone wasn't really a thing, he gripped my breasts hard enough to make me cry out.

One of his hands let go, just for a moment, and then my skin was bare, my top lost to the bed or the floor.

Wherever it was, it could have it.

His lips were on my nipple a heartbeat later, his palms full of my tits. The way he massaged them was intense, but the way he devoured my nipple was something else altogether. He may not have known what he was doing, but he had heard my command to do whatever the hell he wanted to me—and he was definitely doing it.

He sucked, licked, and lathed until I was snarling at him for more. His teeth finally came out, dragging over my nipple, and I cried out, so damn close to the edge. My hips rocked frantically, using his erection to try to push myself over the edge.

Just before I reached it, his hand left my other breast, grabbing my crotch and squeezing it hard in his hand.

I cried out again, so freaking close.

"Let me use you," I snarled.

"You said I could do whatever I want to you." His eyes were silver, his pupils dilated, and his erection was throbbing against my thigh since his hand was blocking me. "I want you to lose it without my cock or fingers. You're close; I can feel it and smell it."

He could *smell* how close I was to shattering?

How—

His lips wrapped around the nipple they hadn't touched yet. Another cry escaped me as I arched into his hand, and my body clenched around nothing.

That bastard didn't know anything about sex, and still took control when I—

His teeth scraped my nipple, and I was gone.

A scream escaped me, my body arching, and arching, and arching as I shuddered through the orgasm.

It was so much more intense than I'd ever realized it could be.

I was panting when my vision finally cleared and found myself still rocking against his palm.

"I want you on your back," the bastard growled at me, his eyes so bright they were glowing as he continued doing exactly what I'd told him to. "I want to see, touch, and taste every inch of you. I want to bring you pleasure with every body part I have. I want to make you so damn insane that my name is the only word you can think anymore."

Holy hell, what had I done?

I opened my mouth to tell him that wasn't what sex was usually like, but before I could say a thing, he had me on my back on the bed, and was stripping my shorts off me.

My gaze caught on his face and followed it down to those massive muscles, to his otherworldly-perfect body.

His huge hands easily parted my thighs, and then he dragged me toward him until my ass was hanging off the edge of the bed. I pulled the pillow with me, so my head was raised enough that I could see—so I could watch him touch me—watch him taste me —watch him work me with his fingers

My core was open wide to the world, every inch of me exposed to the man staring at me so intensely it was a wonder he didn't burst.

A long moment passed before my core clenched at the weight of his attention, and then he moved.

His nose was at the center of me, inhaling deeply, and a savage snarl flooded the room.

When he lifted his gaze, it was silver again, and glowing. "Mine," he said, his chest heaving.

My eyes were practically dinner plates as I stared back at him. He'd done the possessive thing before, but something about claiming me with his eyes full of my core, with his hands holding me open so he could see every inch of me, was so much bigger.

My lips parted, and I intended to tell him to stop. To tell him that I wasn't as invested as he was, that he didn't own me, that I wasn't his.

But then his thumb dragged over my clit, and my brain short-circuited.

And then his tongue dragged up my center, from the top to the very bottom.

In that moment, I probably would've agreed that I belonged to him if it would get me a few more minutes with the man.

But he didn't ask me to agree.

He just devoured me.

His hands parted my center, releasing my thighs, which immediately clamped around his head. He used his tongue, his lips, his teeth, his nose, his fingers... every damn part of him worked my body, feeling my core and rubbing my clit. The scruff on his face burned, but in a way that drove me insane.

I shattered in less than two minutes, my body completely new to being touched and loved the way Calian was doing it. The scream he got out of me was small and hoarse, and the only acknowledgment he gave it was a bite to my clit that made me jerk in his arms.

The pressure was so intense, and he never let up—not when I shattered a third time, or fourth.

I was gasping, sucking in massive breaths of air after the fourth orgasm, and he was still going so hard.

"I want your cock," I snarled at him, my heart pounding and my desperation growing as my breathing started to go ragged again.

"Give me one more." He lifted his glowing gaze from my core for the shortest second.

The way he was looking at me, his face wet with my body's desire, paired with the brutal way he continued to work me, had me screaming again a moment later. This one was different, though— I felt my body gush as the pleasure hit a level I'd never experienced.

Did I just squir—

Calian interrupted my thoughts when he rose to his feet, his grip on my thighs still tight in the best way. His pants were gone, his cock dripping as it bobbed, and his eyes still glowing.

"You are mine," he told me, his voice low as he lined himself up against my entrance.

I was too far gone to listen to his words.

My legs hooked around his ass as he plunged into me, my body arching at the thick, heady pleasure of being filled so completely.

He was huge, and hot, and—

He thrust in and out once, and then again.

I felt like I was being broken and remade again, into something fiercer, hotter, needier, and—

He roared.

The room flooded with fire, and I screamed with him as we lost it together. The pleasure was so much that I saw stars.

Everything smelled burnt when he grabbed me off the bed and pulled me to his chest, his eyes still silver. He was looking at me like a dragon, not just a man—and it was hot.

Or it would've been, if I wasn't so thoroughly spent.

My body felt heavy as he stood, holding me against him.

Electricity danced between us, the magic of our bond probably working in overdrive as it attempted to recharge us after *that*.

"I'm taking you to my mountain," he told me.

I nodded against his chest, pretty damn sure that one or both of us had burned everything in my room, if the smell was any indication.

There was a moment's pause, and then we shot up into the air. Lian shifted as we soared, my body glued to and protected by his as a massive cracking noise sounded.

Had he broken the damn Stronghold?

A moment later, I felt the breeze on my bare skin. I could hear the flap of wings even though I didn't open my eyes to see what was flapping. It had to be Calian—there weren't really any other options.

When I paid attention to the place our skin met, I realized that I felt scales where his skin had been, and I relaxed slightly. He must've been holding me against his lower belly, in his gigantic talons. Enough of my body was covered that I knew I wasn't flashing the world below us.

The rhythmic flapping of his wings lulled me into a thick, heavy sleep.

Thirteen

I woke up with my entire bare, sweaty body plastered to Calian's. His erection dug into my leg, my nose was resting against his neck, and his arms were holding me securely.

It probably should've made me feel trapped.

Instead, I just felt comfortable.

My hair was glued to both of us, the long strands stuck to our skin in random chunks, bits, and pieces. When I tried to move my head, a bunch of different strands tugged right back.

Yep, definitely trapped.

"January?" the big lug mumbled, his voice thick and gravelly.

At least I wasn't the only wrecked one. "What the hell happened?"

"We had sex."

I scowled into his neck. "I remember that part, thanks."

His hands gripped my ass. "Had to make sure."

"What happened afterward?"

"A mating bond, I think. It's a hell of a lot stronger than the ones between the other humans and fae, though."

"Shit," I mumbled.

"I have more power running through my veins than I ever knew was possible. Whatever the connection did, it's far from a bad thing," the man said, his voice low.

It was time to change the subject. "How long have we been out?"

"Sun's rising, so a few hours. My brothers are probably on the way." That last part, he said with a grumble.

"Your brothers?"

"The rest of the Wild Hunt. We're the strongest seelies, so we work together to keep the unseelie bastards on their side of the world. Usually, it's not a big deal. Sometimes it is."

Dammit, there was so much more to this world than I knew. If I was aware of all the right questions to ask, maybe I could start figuring shit out. But I was so damned clueless about so many things.

"Do you have clothes for me?" I checked.

"No. I picked them up after I grabbed your blanket and pillow from here." His hands slid up my bare back, following the curve of it as well as sliding down to my waist.

I wanted to hate the contact, but couldn't.

"Look, about the sex," I began.

Somehow, I had to make sure the bastard and I were on the same page. It was incredible sex, but I was not his wife. I wasn't going to follow his damned orders, live in his house, or do anything else wifely.

He was still mostly a stranger to me.

"Hmm?" His hands slid down my back, dragging over my ass and wrapping around it.

Shit, he was going to make me horny again.

"We had sex, and it was great, and I know we have no control over the mating bond thing you've mentioned so many times, but I'm still not your possession. You can call me whatever you want, but as far as I'm concerned, nothing has really changed."

Except that I was looking forward to having sex with him every day, assuming he was on board. And no way was he stupid enough not to be on board.

He didn't respond, so I went on, "I'm still going to live in the Stronghold. If you broke it, you're going to have to fix it. I'm not moving in with you. We're not a couple. We're just... friends with benefits."

"You say that like it's a term I should know."

"It's a human idea. Friends who have sex. *With benefits* just sounds more polite, I guess."

"Then *with benefits* would be the unseelie way of saying things." His hands squeezed my ass. "I hear what you're saying and respect your opinions."

"My *opinions*?" The annoyance in my voice was thick.

"Yes, *opinions*."

"Screw you," I hissed, rolling off of his body. "I wasn't giving you my opinions, I was telling you what's going to happen between us. You can't force me to be your wife."

The sound of flapping wings cut off our argument.

"We *will* talk about this later," I practically snarled to him, my head jerking around as I tried to establish where I was and where I could find clothes.

There were only three walls around me, and none of them were actual walls. They were slabs of stone, curved and oddly shaped, as if they were part of an overhang that created an almost-cave.

Considering I could see trees out in front of me where the fourth wall should've been, I decided I really was inside some kind of shallow cave.

Calian crossed the room in two strides and grabbed a set of clothes off a rack of sorts that I noticed as soon as he was close to it. He was back at my side in a heartbeat, tugging the gigantic muscle-tee over my head.

"Better keep those breasts hidden," he said playfully, helping me as I shoved my arms through the holes while also glaring at him. "They're mine."

I scoffed as he calmly bent down and held the pants out toward me. Despite my frustration, I shoved my feet into the leg holes. "Better get some pants on that ass," I shot back. "It's *mine*."

The gaze he gave me from where he kneeled in front of me was a hot one, but kind of smirky too. "Yes, it is."

He slid the pants up my thighs. The way he looked at me while he did so made me feel like the fabric was his hands on my skin.

Bastard can't even let me get the upper hand when I sass him.

He was pulling his own pants on when a massive phoenix fell out of the sky, shifting dizzyingly-fast as he spiraled downward. The man landed on his feet without so much as a wince, despite the ridiculous fall he'd just survived. Or performed, I supposed.

It was the jacked guy with the buzzed hair and bicep tattoos, the one who had claimed I was one of his on that first day when they stole me from Earth. His gaze wasn't nearly as intense as it had been when we met, but was now flooded with interest as it swept up and down my figure.

I resisted the urge to wrap my arms around my probably-pointy nipples and instead put my hands on my hips. "What do you want?"

A group of three animals came running and slithering over the ledge the phoenix guy had landed on. My eyes widened as they all shifted back to their male forms. They were all bigger than the creature-forms of any of the fae Lian had introduced me to outside the Stronghold the day before, and if I looked closely at one of them, I could sort of *feel* his magic.

From what I could feel, their magic was really damn strong.

But what could the fae even do with their magic, other than shifting forms?

The fiery bear-dog, which I knew was a hellhound, shifted into the blond, inked-up guy with the feral grin from that first day. The sabertooth-monster shifted into the tight pants guy with the shortish hair. The gigantic snake thing changed into man-bun guy and his short-shorts.

Damn, that was a lot of huge, manly dudes in a small space.

Calian stepped up behind me and wrapped his arm around my waist, pulling my ass back to his erection.

How was he always hard?

"What happened?" the phoenix guy asked, his head tilting sideways a little.

I wondered if I did bird-like shit when I was in my human form.

Part of me expected Calian to give them a savage grin and declare that *sex* had happened, but of course, he didn't.

"My female and I have become one," he said instead. "The bond has settled between us."

"Damn." The sabertooth guy grimaced. "Anyone who didn't have the chance to catch her scent will want you dead."

"I look forward to the fight," Calian said, his voice filling with that savagery I'd been waiting for.

At least it wasn't geared toward sex, though. For now.

"I can't believe you convinced the poor little beast to mate with you so quickly," the hellhound guy drawled. "She seemed so *fiery*."

"*She* is," I growled back. "We had sex. If I had known it was going to mate us, I would've thought twice about it."

That last part was a lie.

It had been so damn good I still would've done it.

But at least then I would've known what I was getting myself into.

"Sex?" The basilisk guy looked at Calian.

"A connection of bodies and souls," Lian replied.

Cryptic bastard.

There was no point in dancing around it. Guess I was explaining it to the other fae after all.

"Men have dicks. Women have vaginas. Dicks fit inside vaginas. When it happens, it's called sex." I gave a shitty explanation but saw the gears in their minds turning.

Had they done something to the other human women to make them stay quiet about it? Or had the women just kept their mouths shut because they didn't know that the fae were so unaware, like the girls back in the Stronghold?

I was going to need to tell them about the whole sex thing when I got back there. No way around that, no matter how much I wanted there to be one.

"Shit," the hellhound guy growled, glancing behind him, as if looking toward the Stronghold.

"If any of those women were meant for you, their scent would have infected every thought that goes through your mind," Lian warned him, his voice low and dangerous.

The hellhound guy growled back, *"Probably,"* but made no move to turn around. I remembered what Calian had said, about the leaders thinking that mate connections could possibly happen over time too, even though they hadn't proven it.

"None of my people had a chance," the sabertooth guy said, his voice lowering. "When they hear about sex, they will come for you."

"I'll await it eagerly," Lian drawled.

A snort escaped the phoenix guy, and I jerked my head toward him as he said, "Your power feels like mine now, brother."

Calian's chuckle made my shoulders relax slightly. "It feels different. Both phoenix and dragon." He held out an arm, and I watched fire dance along it. The flames looked different than they had the day before—less like his and more like mine. "What do the borders look like?"

"No sign of unseelies yet, but they'll be sending a party to check after the disturbance of your mating. You should meet them there."

Lian dipped his head in a nod. "We'll head there after we pick up clothes from the Stronghold."

I was going to be meeting unseelies at the border between their lands?

That sounded kind of awesome.

"I saw the hole you left in its roof, brother," the phoenix remarked with a bit of a grin. "Do you have someone to fix it yet?"

"Not yet. I'm sure there's a line of volunteers outside, though."

"I'll do it," the sabertooth guy said.

"I'll help," the basilisk added.

Now that they'd heard about sex, I figured the bastards wanted another chance to sniff around the ladies inside the Stronghold. I'd warn the other girls before we left them alone with the Wild Hunt bastards, if I had the chance.

"Thank you." Calian nodded toward them, and both men nodded back.

They both turned and headed back into the forest, shifting smoothly as they went. I couldn't imagine what it would be like to feel so in tune with my animal side that I'd shift as easily and quickly as they did, but something about the idea sounded really damn appealing to me.

"Get out of here. I need a minute with my female before we fly for the border," Lian growled at them, his voice taking on a bit of teasing.

"We'll hold it for you. Enjoy, brother." The hellhound guy smirked before he too turned and shifted.

The phoenix fae studied us for a few long moments before he shifted and took off into the air, fire licking the space he had been a moment earlier as he vanished into the sky.

"Do powerful bastards always get together and team up?" I asked Lian. I couldn't decide whether the group of them reminded me of prison, my foster homes, or my high school.

"Like attracts like." The man shrugged. "If you don't have family, it's because you haven't found the right people yet."

He had no idea how hard his words hit me, but my throat swelled anyway.

I didn't say a damn thing as I stepped away from him.

"Leave the clothes here so you don't burn them in your shift," he instructed me, watching me closely. Maybe he could tell that my mood had changed.

"Yes sir," I muttered, tugging my top off first.

The way his damned gaze trailed over my skin made my cheeks flush, but I ignored the heat.

My pants joined the shirt, and then I jogged out the cave's opening, seeking the power I felt thrumming lightly in my veins. When I found the sensation, I focused on it, and the beat picked up faster.

The change took over my body, and warmth flooded me as I shifted forms. A grin stretched my cheeks before they shifted, my shape morphing as the fire and liquid gold of the creature I'd become took hold of me.

My wings spread, and I lifted my chin at the powerful stretch of them.

Damn, I was something incredible.

"My gorgeous mate," a male voice murmured. The sentence wasn't spoken aloud, but was somehow in my mind, or within me.

My heartbeat picked up.

"Tell me I did not just hear you in my head," I shot back.

Lian's low, gravelly chuckle was the only response I got back.

My wings pumped hard, carrying me into the sky, and my eyes closed as the thick, powerful wind rushed against my face, my burning feathers, and the thick legs hanging below me.

There was *nothing* as amazing as flying.

"You're perfect, January." Lian's voice touched my mind again.

The words made me shudder, even in my phoenix form.

"Don't," I whispered back. *"You have no idea who I am or what I've done. My life has been very, very different than yours."*

"And yet you fly before me, strong, certain, and powerful. Your past has little to do with your present perfection."

The pure certainty in his voice was enough to make my chest hurt. *"Just stop."*

He didn't speak again, but through whatever magic connected us, I could somehow *feel* his curiosity about why I was so against his compliments.

We flew the rest of the way in silence. Eventually, I relaxed again, despite the reminders of my past that his words had dredged up.

When he knew the hell I'd survived and the damage I'd done, he would never call me perfect.

Fourteen

My eyes squinted as we approached the Stronghold. The longer I stared at the small gap in the trees, the more I thought I could actually make out the hidden building within.

That was insane—it was invisible.

"You only need to be in tune with the building's magic to see it, Love," Calian murmured to me.

My chest clenched. *"Don't call me that."*

His chuckle brushed my mind, and he otherwise didn't acknowledge my words.

We landed in front of it. While Lian shifted in the air before he landed on two feet, I had to hit the ground and focus on getting myself back into my human form before I managed to shift back.

By the time I was back in my skin, the man's front was pressed up against my back, his arms around my chest and waist to keep my lady bits out of the sight of the other men around us.

A few of them yelled as Calian ushered me into the building—the door of which opened just in time to let us in.

Sunny slammed the door behind us with an unceremonious *oof* and leaned her back against it. She flashed me a wild grin. "This place got so much more exciting when you got here."

A snort escaped me. "You're welcome, I guess."

Her grin widened. "Next time you're going to have screaming-hot sex with a gigantic fae, mind warning us so we can get out of here? Or taking it back to wherever that bastard lives? I'm all for the sex, but would rather not hear about all the excitement I'm missing."

My face flushed, and an awkward laugh escaped me. "Sorry. Will do."

"Don't apologize for getting some. I wouldn't say no to hot fae sex myself." She glanced over her shoulder at the door behind her.

Lian's arms tightened around me.

She hadn't clarified which gigantic fae she expected me to be having sex with, which his mind told me he didn't like one bit.

"Be careful, they're clingy," I called to Sunny, as the gigantic fae hauled me to my bedroom. Her laughter made my lips curve upward a bit, even as Lian slammed the door.

He set me down and stared at me with narrowed eyes. "Your humans aren't monogamists?"

"Most are. Some aren't. It's complicated." I shrugged.

"Should you touch another man, I will destroy him." Lian's eyes went silver and got all glowy. "You are *mine*."

"Stop. I'm not planning on having sex with another fae, alright?" I tossed a hand in the direction the other fae were gathered. "I don't consider us married, like you do, but I do understand your clinginess and the permanence of our connection. Besides that, I have no desire to touch any of your buddies. So just... stop."

The glow in his eyes faded slightly.

I finally turned away from him and looked around the room.

Shit.

The blanket and sheets I'd loved were totally roasted. The walls had taken on a blackish hue. The floor was covered in bits of dust that I imagined was something that had been charcoaled. The ceiling had a wide hole in it, and leaves and dirt had already started falling in through the thing.

"Damn," I mumbled.

The only things that didn't look at all singed were the fireproof outfits lined up in the closet.

Sadness and irritation engulfed me, and I tried to ignore them as I slid into the closet and tugged one of the sets of black fireproof lingerie over my skin, covering my tits and ass, but not solving my new attitude problem.

I'd loved that room.

It was mine.

And...

Well, it was wrecked.

I pushed hair out of my eyes and shoved my sadness away.

I should've expected to lose the place; I always lost everything. Hoping for a different outcome was an utter waste.

My stomach was clenched when I stepped out of the closet and found Calian studying me with narrowed eyes.

If he said something judgy, I was going to go off on him.

"Let's go," I growled at him.

There was no point in looking for the door when we had a gigantic hole.

I shifted forms and then launched myself up into the air, tucking my wings in tight before I shot up through the hole. The stone scraped my body hard enough that I smelled a little blood, but I welcomed the pain.

I'd started letting myself get way too comfortable.

Nothing in Vevol was guaranteed any more than it had been on Earth.

Nothing was safe.

Nothing was certain.

Dropping my guard was so stupid. I should never have let Lian touch me, or considered a friendship with benefits for us.

If I was going to survive, the only person I could trust was myself.

"You're upset," the dragon said to me, as we flew. He'd taken the lead, and since I didn't know where we were going, I didn't try to argue with him about it.

"Back off," I snarled back.

He said nothing, though I could feel the bastard's curiosity seeping through our stupid connection once again as we continued to fly.

I'd cooled off a little by the time we reached the place he said was the border between the two fae lands. It was a valley within the massive range of vibrantly-colored mountains, and he told to me that the curve of the valley stretched along the entirety of their world. I had no idea how big said world was compared to Earth, and when I asked him, Calian didn't have an answer. He just said that it took about a day to fly the circumference of Vevol.

We landed off to the side of a thick stone building that was shaped like a gigantic triangle, and was surrounded by melted snow. My claws sliced through the snow without feeling any of the chill, but when they shifted back to feet, my toes curled at the iciness engulfing them.

Then my feet burst into flames—I could feel the fire coming from within me and my thrumming magic—and the ice melted into a steaming puddle. My body relaxed, and for a minute, I felt like I was in a sauna.

Calian's hand captured mine. When I looked at him, I realized he had put on a pair of shorts that reminded me of the hellhound and phoenixes. I'd only seen two pairs of them in his cave, so I didn't think he was a huge fan of the things, but I had told him to cover up.

The fact that he respected my wishes felt important, so I shoved it away and tried to pull my hand out of his.

"You're free to be angry with me, but while we're on neutral territory, you must act like you've accepted that you're mine," the dragon said into my mind. I stopped trying to tug my hand out of his, but didn't grip him as securely as he did me.

I didn't know he could do so while we were in our person forms, and grimaced now that I knew.

"Why?" I asked, my voice snappier than I intended.

"The unseelie have many rules. If they believe I'm trying to force you to be my mate, they will attempt to take you from me, and our people will go to war. They believe in control, in all of its uncomfortable

forms. Our wildness is savagery in their eyes, rather than the freedom it feels like to us."

My throat constricted a little.

As much as I hated to admit it, I understood what he was saying. I too had been around people who tried to enforce stupid, pointless rules that only served to make those who had created them feel more powerful.

And I too had found freedom in the seelies' wildness.

So I tightened my grip on his hand.

"This doesn't mean I've decided to be your wife," I growled at the man whose hand I gripped like a lifeline.

"Of course not," he said, his low chuckle making me warmer than I wanted to admit.

Despite our disagreements, we walked into the triangle-shaped building like we were united.

My gaze skimmed over the group of men waiting inside, all of them with their arms folded as they glared at each other. Among them, there were two that I knew and four that I didn't.

The two I knew were the hellhound guy and the phoenix dude—the four that I didn't know were all unseelies, but I recognized them for what they were because they all had on matching button-up shirts and slacks, none of which looked comfortable to me. The basilisk guy who had come to pick Ana up on that first day wasn't among them, but he had been wearing the same thing when he showed up to get her.

"Brothers," Calian said, his voice a lot less warm as he spread an arm toward them—the arm that wasn't wrapping around my waist and pulling my body closer to his with every step we took.

I didn't turn to eye him, hiding my surprise at the sudden change in his personality.

Was he putting on some kind of a mask for them?

Hadn't I done that dozens of times as a kid, when shit would change and I would need to change with it to survive?

The men seemed to call each other "brothers" a lot, but only with the other members of the Wild Hunt had I seen Calian actually seem to mean the word.

"Lian." One of the men watched me, his eyes piercing.

"You must not be too concerned, since you haven't brought the full council," Calian drawled back.

I was officially as nestled against him as was possible, his entire front glued to my whole back. The man seemed partial to holding me that way, and honestly, I liked it.

Not that I'd admit it to him.

"Druze and Ashvyn are dealing with the little female *problem* you handed us," one man countered. Something about the plethora of tattoos on his dark skin and the way he held himself reminded me of the hellhound guy a few feet to my right.

"You made the five-year rule, not us," Calian replied.

"And you know we couldn't have taken them any sooner," the growly guy countered.

The blond hellhound dude grinned. "Careful, Rien. Your hound is showing."

"Wouldn't want to let anyone see the beast you hide away so carefully," Lian agreed, that infuriating smirk so evident in his voice.

"Enough playing, *Calian*." The man who spoke emphasized my dragon's full name, something the other men must not have known until Calian gave it to me, if I understood the name-secrecy properly. If he had known it, I assumed Lian would've been snarling at him or trying to kill him or something. "Aren't you going to introduce us to your little phoenix?"

Being called his little phoenix was insulting, but I held my tongue and settled on glaring back at the man.

"My mate, you mean?" Lian squeezed my hip playfully. "Don't tell me you're jealous, brother. It's been far too long since any of our people found a compatible human—and it's pretty apparent none have been as lucky as I am."

Dammit.

The bastard was going to flaunt the fact that we'd had sex, wasn't he?

The man's eyes burned into him. "I felt the shift in Vevol when your bond solidified. That didn't happen with the rest of us, so what did you do?"

"He fucked his mate." The blond hellhound guy smirked. "Apparently, our bodies are meant to intertwine with a female's."

I was going to kill all of them.

The Wild Hunt was going to die.

End of the damn discussion.

"She's glaring at you like you've spilled her gender's most closely-kept secret," one of the unseelie bastards remarked. His gaze flicked to me. "The other females will hate you, I'm sure."

The question was a taunt, but it was utter bullshit.

"Sex isn't a secret. If you've got twenty women here and none of them have ever tried to screw one of you, it's because you're ugly bastards. Your fault, not mine." I flashed him one of his awful smirks.

The man was just as gorgeous as the rest of them, but they didn't need to know that.

"Looks like Vevol made a wise match. A fire-tongued she-devil to go with the Savage King." The hellhound who I was pretty sure had been called Rien glared at us.

"And nothing but loneliness for the cold, unseelie council," our hellhound replied.

I wasn't sure when I'd started thinking of myself as one of the seelie, but it was too late to change my mind. I was one of them— whether I liked it or not.

"You can smell that our scents have merged. Whether or not the female could've been anyone else's, she belongs to me. Take that news back to your king and his icy mate." Lian's fingers pressed lightly into my skin, and I understood the silent push.

We were moving, right then.

I turned as he guided me, walking in front of him and not saying a damn thing when he blocked my ass from their sight with his ginormous body.

"You know this could be the start of a war between us," one of the men called from behind me and Calian. "Your people can't support this. You're too wild—and too reckless."

"Bring us the war, and you'll see just how wild and reckless we can be," Calian's phoenix friend said.

I felt more than heard the seelie hound and phoenix following us out of the building.

"Are they really going to start a war over us getting accidentally mated?" I whispered to Calian, when we were far enough from them that I knew they wouldn't hear me.

"Probably not. But if they do, our people will fight, and we will win. The one thing we all agree on is the freedom we deserve," the dragon told me. "Shift, Precious."

I about gagged at the nickname, and heard him snort at my reaction even as his form shifted.

Mine followed soon after his, and faster than I would've thought possible a few days earlier, we were in the air.

Fifteen

We flew all the way back to the Stronghold, and Calian left me to my thoughts. I wasn't sure where my mind was at—mostly, it was just a mess.

Everything had happened too quickly, and I was past overwhelmed. If Lian could read my emotions the way I had started to be able to read his, he would realize that and back the hell off.

When we got to the Stronghold, the phoenix guy circled overhead, and the hellhound one followed us to the door, snarling and snapping at the other men waiting outside. He stood behind us while we waited for one of the other ladies to get the door. When Dots pulled it open, eyeing the guys behind us, the hellhound guy dipped his head and gave us a feral grin before he took off into the trees.

The door closed behind us, and Calian made quick work of the locks. Not as quickly as Ana had that first day, but he didn't have the same experience.

"So?" Sunny demanded as we walked into the living room. She, Mare, and Dots occupied a couch, and were clutching their pillows and blankets with excitement.

I guessed things usually got pretty boring in the Stronghold.

"Tell us everything," Dots ordered.

My instincts were to clam up and hide out, but that wasn't how shit worked in the Stronghold. And the girls there... well, I wanted to be close with them, like they were with each other.

I liked them, even if it might have been a shitty call on my part.

So, I ignored my instincts, collapsing onto a couch. When Calian dropped next to me and pulled half of me up onto his lap, I let him.

I had to pick my battles with that bastard, after all.

I told the other girls everything that had happened and everything that I'd learned. About the fae not knowing what sex was—that one shocked the hell out of them and led to way too much laughter—about the Wild Hunt guys, about the seelie versus the unseelie... everything I'd heard, which turned out to be a hell of a lot more than they'd learned in their time in Vevol.

Then again, I'd had a front-row seat, while they'd been safely tucked away in the Stronghold.

When I finally finished explaining and headed to the kitchen for something to eat, I noticed North leaning up against the doorway of her room, her eyes narrowed but not angry as she stared at me.

She must've come out when she realized what we were talking about.

When she realized that I'd noticed her standing there, she spun around and stormed back into her room, slamming the door hard behind her.

I shrugged it off.

Calian cooked for all of us—I was pretty sure I was going to have to fight Mare, Dots, and Sunny for the bastard if he kept doing that—and then he and I retired to our room. I tossed my middle finger over my head when Sunny hollered to keep the sex quiet this time, and ignored my burning cheeks.

I was exhausted, and having a full stomach only made me want to sleep even more.

When the door was closed behind us and we were alone in my room, it took me a minute to look around and see what had happened. Someone had fixed the hole in the roof—Lian's friends, I assumed—and left a new sheet and blanket tossed haphazardly over a fresh mattress. The ashes or whatever had been on the ground had been swept up and removed. Even though the scorch marks remained on the walls and floors, the space smelled clean.

"Damn," I murmured, taking everything in.

Lian was already putting the sheet on the bed, the thick blanket draped over his shoulder.

"You have good friends," I admitted to him. "Or brothers, I guess. What are their names?"

Calian dropped the mattress and tossed the blanket over the bed. "The hellhound is Priel. He's a bastard, but the most loyal fae you can find. Ervo is the phoenix. He's the most intelligent of us, notices every detail that the rest of us miss, but he's private. I know less about him than the others, despite the centuries we've known each other." He waved me over, and I slowly, reluctantly, shuffled toward him. "Nev is the basilisk. He's a sneaky asshole, but could make a damned forest mouse laugh."

"A forest mouse?" My voice was dubious.

"This big. Fuzzy." He moved his hands in about the same size as a loaf of bread.

Shit, I did *not* want to meet one of those mice.

"Mean bastards. Sharp teeth, hard to kill, foul meat." He shrugged. "Teris is the sabertooth. He'd sooner start a fight than have a logical conversation, which is both his best and worst quality."

I snorted, and Calian's lips tilted up slightly. I finally reached him, and his hands wrapped around my hips, drawing me closer until I was nestled between his thighs. I felt tiny in his arms, and didn't hate that feeling at all. "And what about you?" I asked him.

"What about me?"

"If I was asking them the same question about you, what would they tell me?"

He grimaced. "That I'm the obnoxious one, I suppose. In everyone's business. Won't leave the bastards alone. Showing up with food, forcing them to get up and do shit when they want to be alone."

Well, that didn't sound obnoxious to me.

Not at all.

"What kind of food?" I checked.

"Cake, usually. Who do you think told the bastards outside that they should bring treats when they wanted to convince the human women to talk to them?"

I snorted. "That was actually a great idea."

"Thank you." His lips curved up further. "What would your friends say about you, January?"

My humor died. "I don't have friends. Friends are just people who pretend to like you until they're ready to screw you over."

"I'm sorry." Something about his gaze felt far too much like the pity I'd never wanted from any of the many people who had pitied me throughout my life. "Are you ready for bed?"

I stepped out of his grip, and he released me, though I felt the reluctance in the way his touch lingered. "I want to be alone tonight. I need space to think. Time, too. Everything's happened too fast since I got here."

His jaw clenched and his eyes narrowed. "Space?"

"Yes, space." I stared back at him, my eyes just as narrow as his. "I still haven't agreed to be your wife, remember? You were probably hoping for sex, but you're going to have to deal with space instead."

His eyes flashed silver. "Should I walk out the Stronghold's doors, I'm going to have to fight the fae who believe you could've been theirs had they met you first."

"Then you probably have a few friends out there, waiting to fight with you," I shot back.

His silent glare was all the answer I needed.

"We just met, Lian. I don't know you. You don't know me. There's more to a relationship than sex, and we don't even have a relationship. If I need to go out there and let them all sniff me so you don't have to kill anyone, that's fine, I'll do it. But you don't just get to *assume* that we're going to be together constantly now."

His jaw clenched further. "Alright. I'll spend the night making sure none of the bastards outside get in here, so you can have your *space*."

I knew for a fact that the Stronghold had been built to keep the fae out—and I was fairly confident none of them would harm us. If they intended to do that, there would've been at least some sign.

But I didn't say that.

I only jerked my head in a nod. "Fine."

Calian stood stiffly, and my eyes followed him as he crossed the room.

His muscles were tense as he tugged the door open, and my teeth cut into my lip.

The door slammed behind him, and I released a heavy rush of air.

My chest hurt, and I didn't want to think about why.

I considered going out to the living room, to watch a movie with the other girls, but I didn't want them to cheer me up. Something told me they would.

So instead, I locked the door and collapsed on the bed.

It smelled wrong.

I hated that.

But I'd slept in dozens of beds that smelled wrong, so I ignored my emotions for the umpteenth time, and shoved my body under the blankets.

Sleep.

Sleep would be good.

It took way longer than I wanted it to, but I finally managed to drift off.

· · ·

WHEN I WOKE UP, I felt physically fine but mentally and emotionally exhausted.

I stumbled out of bed and into the kitchen, even though I wasn't really hungry.

Dots and Mare were sitting at our dinner table, playing a game that looked like Scrabble. I was shitty at Scrabble, and grumpy enough that seeing them play it made me scowl.

"Don't go outside. Looks like a crime scene out there," Dots murmured to me. "I didn't see any bodies, at least."

My chest tightened painfully, and I muttered a thanks as I grabbed some kind of weird-ass fruit. I'd seen the other girls eat it like an apple, even though the shape was like a pear and a star had a love-child and the skin looked like a lizard's.

I bit into it, and glared at the damn thing when it tasted incredible.

My back rested against one of the cabinets, and I stared daggers at the fridge while I ate. The girls behind me finished their game and then cleaned up and headed to their rooms, saying something about showering.

After a few minutes, North stalked out of her room. Almost all of her skin was still covered, and she glared at me like always.

This time, I glared back.

Neither of us said a word to each other as she grabbed a pear-star thing for herself.

She headed back toward her room, but stopped halfway. I didn't glance over when she returned, her fist wrapped around her alien pear.

"You're not the only one who's had a hard life," she snarled at me. Fire danced in the orbs of her eyes, and I fought to keep my shock off my face. "If you're going to be a bitch, stay in your room."

With that, she stormed back across the living area. Her bedroom door slammed behind her.

There was a long moment of silence before I finally sighed to myself.

I *was* being a bitch.

Being in a shitty mood and questioning everything I knew and felt didn't mean I had to act like a damn storm cloud.

Was that why North stayed in *her* room?

Because she'd had a hard life and didn't want to make everyone else as miserable as she was?

I didn't know if we'd ever be friends, but that short interaction already made me see her differently.

I shuffled over to one of the couches and took a seat, tucking my legs up onto the couch next to me and then tugging a blanket over them. My anger chilled a little as I worked on my lizard-fruit, staring at one of the bookshelves like it held the answers to everything.

Though I knew it didn't have a damn thing for me, it felt good to hope.

Mare came back out of her room a bit later, wearing a clean pair of clothes and smelling kind of like the fruit I was eating. She flashed me a quick, small smile as she pulled a book off the shelf. It looked well-loved, and I wondered how many times she had read it. Or, had it been one of the previous women's favorites?

"You okay?" she asked me, distracting me from my thoughts.

"I don't know," I admitted.

Mare took a seat on the couch that I'd noticed she frequented—the thing was practically her own. "Want to talk about it?"

"I..." I bit my lip.

Talking about things only ever made them worse for me, but I did know that for some people, talking shit out was how they worked through it. Therapists wouldn't have jobs if it didn't, right? And I'd never met a therapist I actually liked, but plenty of people had, so they couldn't *all* be bad.

Theoretically.

"Calian thinks we're married," I admitted. "I've never even had a boyfriend. He was smothering me, and I liked it, but I was afraid of how much I liked it. That probably sounds stupid, but..." I sighed. "I don't know."

"It's not stupid. Not many people would be able to go from a life they hated in a world they didn't want to be in, to a new world where a man considered her the love of his life without a little stress. Or a lot of stress."

I groaned. "You make it sound even worse."

She laughed. "Knowing it's a weird situation just makes you more capable of dealing with it, January."

January.

"Why do you guys all call me that? I've never gone by my full name in my entire life. My first foster parents thought it was too weird."

She gave me a small smile. "It just fits you. Back on Earth, January is a fresh start. A new year. We've all experienced January so many times, but every time it comes around, people still walk into it with new goals they want to accomplish and ideas about the new person they want to become. January is just... hope, I guess. You might not be a super hopeful person, but you're a survivor. Anyone can see that, Calian included, I can imagine. And there's something innately hopeful about looking at someone and seeing that they survived shit that would break most people."

I grimaced. "Survival *definitely* broke me."

She shook her head, biting her lip and looking out a window. "I..." she trailed off, and her gaze lingered on the window the girls had uncovered a few days earlier. "When things were bad, I read books. I hid in worlds that never existed. I always have, and I probably always will. I didn't survive things, I just... ignored them. Pretended they weren't real. I'm not proud of that, either. The only thing I've done that I'm actually, genuinely proud of was wishing on the star that opened the portal for the Wild Hunt to bring me here, and I almost didn't do that. So yeah, I respect you, and I don't think you're broken. You look your demons in the eyes, and I don't. That's something I've always wished I could change about myself."

"Keeping your head down isn't hiding from your problems. It's another survival tactic, one I've always wished I was better at," I argued, leaning toward her. My lizard-fruit was still in one hand, two-thirds eaten and yet forgotten at the same time. "There's nothing shameful about choosing not to pick a fight."

"*Those who stand for nothing fall for everything*," Mare said quietly. "No one really knows who said that quote, but it feels like it was written about my life."

I didn't know that I'd ever heard her swear before, and I kind of loved it.

"*Live to fight another day,*" I countered. "I have no idea who said that one, but I think it's a much better summary of your life, and I don't even know what kind of life you've lived."

A snort escaped her. "I wish you were wrong."

"Well, I usually am. So don't get used to this." I leaned back against the couch, fighting a soft smile I never usually showed.

We were both quiet for a few minutes.

Mare broke the silence, though her voice was soft. "Have you told Lian that you want to take things slow and get to know each other? In the years I've been here, he's checked up on us more than all of the other fae put together. He takes care of people. If you explain to him that you're not ready for the kind of relationship he wants, but that you might be in a few weeks, or months, or years, I can't imagine he would walk away."

I bit my lip, considering it.

She was right; I didn't have a damned doubt about that.

Lian would take whatever I gave him, even if he was pissed about doing so.

"He deserves more, you know? Like... he's not innocent; he's probably killed a hundred fae."

"At least," Mare agreed.

I sighed heavily. "Not innocent, but not experienced in the ways I am. I don't think this world has the kind of darkness that I've seen back on Earth, honestly. And I don't want it to, but that makes it hard for me to consider a relationship with someone who can't understand me."

"Can't, or hasn't been given the chance?" Mare countered.

I shot her a glare. "Why do you have to make me think about these things?"

A laugh escaped her. "You're the one trying to force me to reconsider my whole outlook on life. Live to fight another day, my ass."

A smile teased my lips. "Fine, so we both need to shape up. That's not new for me."

"Me either, unfortunately." She flashed me a small grin. "I'll give it a try if you will."

"I'm going to hold it against you if it doesn't work," I warned her.

She laughed again. "Is that a promise?"

I offered her a hand, and she reached out and shook it.

It felt like more than a promise to try to get out of our comfort zones, honestly.

It felt like... friendship.

Sixteen

Despite my conversation with Mare, I put off a real talk with Calian for a few days. He brought cake every day, and we both ignored the bits of dried blood on his various body parts every time. The bastard even came in to cook for me twice a day, something the other ladies definitely didn't complain about.

I didn't ask any serious questions other than making sure the unseelie weren't starting a war yet (they weren't), and he didn't push me for more. It was... honestly, pretty nice, even though we both knew we were avoiding the elephant in the room.

The other ladies and I spent our days playing games of poker with rocks for chips—all of us losing horribly to a grinning Sunny—as well Scrabble, which Dots and Mare alternated winning, and long games of Monopoly. I never won any of them, but to my surprise, I didn't mind. Having people to play games with was something new for me, and honestly, I was kind of falling in love with it.

A week had gone by before I shuffled to the bathroom one morning and blearily blinked at my reflection.

It took me a minute to really look at myself, but when I did, my jaw fell open.

Thin, elegant golden markings had appeared all over both of my arms. I spun quickly, looking at my back in the mirror, and ripped my tank top off so I could see the magical tattoos better.

They climbed over my shoulders and up my neck, then stretched down my back and wrapped around my ass and thighs.

When I gaped down at my legs, I found more of the golden ink stretching across my skin.

"Holy shit," I whispered to myself, my gaze glued to my arms and legs, following the gorgeous markings. "Holy shit!" I suddenly understood why people did victory dances after they won things.

It was *awesome*. The markings were unique, and gorgeous, and fun—it was like the world's magic had heard my desire for tattoos and answered it!

My heart beat quickly in my chest, excitement thrumming with the fire magic in my veins.

I didn't know it could take that long—was my body still changing?

It didn't matter.

I was excited—and there was one person I wanted to tell above the others.

I rushed toward the door out of my room, but halted abruptly before I could open it.

Shit.

Why was Calian the first person I wanted to tell?

That felt like a bad sign, that I wanted to tell him more than I wanted to tell the other girls. I had been spending plenty of time with all of them except North, but my mind always seemed to go back to the time Lian and I spent flying—and screwing—and just... talking.

Yeah, I was really thinking it was a bad sign.

Was I starting to like the big bastard as more than a friend? Or more than a friend-with-benefits that I'd only *benefited* from once?

"Friends like to tell each other things," I told myself aloud. "It's normal. Natural. Not something to stress about."

Now I was being insane, talking to myself, but whatever.

Wanting to tell Calian about my new tattoos was fine. It was just because we were friends.

Yep, I was going with that.

As I stepped outside my room, I forced myself to slow down, since we were just friends and all.

None of the other girls were up yet, but I was confident that Lian would be awake and outside. As far as I could tell, he hadn't gone back to his cave to change once since I told him I needed space.

I opened the last few locks on the doors—we'd been leaving most of them undone to save time—and tugged it open before slipping outside. The air was slightly chilly in the mornings, but it felt good against my always-warm skin now that I was a phoenix.

Calian was in his massive dragon form, his body stretched out in front of the door, preventing anyone from leaving or entering.

So much for needing the locks.

The dragon turned and lifted his head, looking slightly surprised that I was outside that early. Because I had been avoiding serious conversations, I'd been forced to avoid flying and spending any time alone with the man as well, so I'd sort of been hiding out in the Stronghold.

"Look," I whispered, excitement probably showing through my voice even though I was trying not to act like a damned puppy.

His body shifted as his gaze dragged over my skin. "The magic has finally set in completely." His voice was a rough murmur, and I was fairly certain I'd pulled him out of sleep. "It suits you beautifully."

My face flushed.

Yeah, that was what I'd been hoping he'd say. I wasn't about to admit that out loud, but it was the truth.

"Thanks."

"You'll have nature magic within you now, too. When you're ready to learn how to use it, let me know."

Nature magic?

Was that the power I could feel coming off of the fae so often? Was it how the Wild Hunt guys had managed to fix my roof so quickly and so perfectly, or why Calian lived in a cave?

There were so many questions I wanted to ask, but asking them would mean accepting the bond between us in a way that I wasn't sure I could handle.

So I didn't ask.

Instead, I bit down on my lip.

This was...

Not what I'd hoped.

His comments were everything, but when I'd come out of the room, I'd just...

I don't know.

Wanted more, I guess.

Maybe I didn't want as much space as I thought I did.

A bird cawed loudly overhead, and my chin lifted as I tried to peer up into the sky, through the thick tree branches above our heads.

"It's Ervo," Lian told me, stepping closer but not putting his hands on my skin.

I suddenly missed them violently, those days when he'd touched me every chance he got.

"What does he want?" I asked.

"I don't know."

A brief moment of silence passed, and then a massive phoenix dropped out of the sky.

My stomach clenched at the sight of him, and the thrumming power in my chest went a bit wild.

It had been too long since I'd been in my own phoenix form— since I'd had the chance to fly.

"The unseelie council is in the valley. They've come to negotiate in hopes of avoiding a war," the phoenix said, not bothering with a hello or any other pleasantries.

"The rest of our brothers?" Lian asked.

"On their way as we speak. We've warned our men to be ready for a battle, as well."

Calian dipped his head in a nod. "I'll let mine know and meet you there."

"May the winds favor you." Ervo nodded toward me, a silent, polite greeting, before he launched himself back into the air, shifting and taking to the skies.

"What will they ask for?" I looked at Calian.

"No way to predict with the unseelies." His gaze lingered on me. "I'll return and let you know as soon as I can."

Whoa, what?

I grabbed his arm before he threw himself up into the sky like Ervo had.

"You're not seriously going to leave me here." My voice was somewhere between surprised and offended.

"You wished for space. I won't take you in front of the unseelies while you're uncomfortable touching me; any sign of weakness will only encourage them."

Shit.

"You think I'm uncomfortable touching you?" My voice had a weird lilt that I didn't know what to think about.

"That seems clear, yes."

My throat swelled a bit.

This was an important moment between us—I could feel it.

I hadn't realized he thought I was uncomfortable around him. If I didn't do something to prove that I wasn't, that feeling would stick around for him.

If I did... then I would be removing the space I'd forced him to put between us.

My conversation with Mare came to mind, and in that instant, my choice was made.

I covered the distance between us in a heartbeat, burying my hands in the back of his hair and pressing my lips to his.

Lian gave me a moment to take it back, a moment to step away, before his massive hands swallowed my hips and his tongue was in my mouth, his lips devouring mine.

Our bodies were plastered together, interlocked as much as they could be without any privacy.

And damn, I'd missed kissing him.

He kissed me like I was his everything, and held me like he was afraid he might lose me.

And the fact he felt that way, that he cared about me as much as he did, was staggering.

Damn, I loved it.

Calian walked me backward as he kissed me, until my shoulders met the firm, somewhat-invisible barrier of the Stronghold. His hands slid down my thighs, caressing my skin in a way that made me want him so much I could hardly stand it. Then he grabbed them, hauling me up and pinning my pelvis against his. His erection ground against my core, and I groaned into his mouth.

Maybe I'd spoken too soon about the whole *without privacy* thing.

His fingers slid inside my shorts, wrapping possessively around my ass cheeks and spreading me wider.

I ripped my face away from his, the back of my head knocking into the wall as I panted, "Wait."

His fingers clenched my ass, his silver eyes burning into me.

"We have an audience, probably." I jerked my head toward the forest.

His head whipped around, his eyes narrowing.

His fingers tightened on my ass again, the grip so tight it hurt a little, but in the best way.

"And the unseelies want a war. We have to talk to them. Afterward..." I bit my lip. "We can go back to your cave for a day or two."

His eyes darkened, and he dipped his head in a nod.

Lian's lips captured mine again, and he gave me one last scorching kiss before he tossed me over his back, shifting before I collided with his warm skin, and took off into the air.

My magic pulsed in my chest as we picked up speed and altitude. Flying had come naturally to me when I shifted, but there was no doubt that Lian was faster. He had done it a hell of a lot more than I had, and he was just plain old massive.

Maybe I'd eventually be able to keep pace with him, but at the moment, I was content with the fact that he could outfly me.

Despite the magic and my own yearning to shift, I felt through our bond that Calian wanted me where I was. I'd been avoiding paying attention to the connection ever since I told him I wanted space, but his emotions had still brushed against my mind every now and then. They did so enough to let me know how difficult it had been for him to give me the space I needed.

And now that we were touching again, they let me know that he needed me to remain in physical contact with him.

It was a strange thought, that he needed me.

I'd never been needed before.

As much as I hated to admit it, I liked it.

We flew for a few hours, and the more time I spent snuggled up on Calian's back, the more I started to wonder if space was what I had ever wanted from the man at all.

SEVENTEEN

EVENTUALLY, we landed in the valley. I slid off Calian's back before he could grab me, managing to crash to my feet instead of the ground. When he landed beside me in his man form, his arm wrapped securely around my waist. I leaned in closer to him without thinking about it, and when I did think about it, accepted that I just wanted to be close to him.

"They don't know what to think of you," he murmured to me as we walked. "That's an advantage for us. If you feel it can help at any point, speak up. No need to hide your opinions or hold yourself back."

My eyebrows shot upward.

No one had ever told me not to hide what I was. That was the name of the game in foster care; they wanted us to become someone entirely different so we'd appeal to the *bleeding hearts* who might eventually want to adopt us. I had hated that so much —the insistence to be on our best behavior and show respect even if the potential families treated us like garbage. Sure, maybe some of them actually might have been good people, but I'd lived with more than a few who were just in it to make money off of us.

"You don't want me to stay quiet?" I asked, as we reached the entrance to the pyramid-shaped building.

"Not unless you prefer to." He squeezed my hip lightly, and our eyes met.

The contact made me bite my lip to suppress a wave of emotions I couldn't control or understand.

We stepped into the building, and I let my gaze trail over the room.

It was the same as it had been before, but there were a few more people inside. Three unseelie men I didn't recognize—one of which was wearing a crown that was just as big as his gigantic head. It gleamed like some kind of black metal, but my attention didn't linger on it.

It lingered on the woman next to him.

She was tall and willowy, with piercing blue eyes and thick, dark hair. Her skin was a dark tan color, and one of her arms was coated in spiraling letters that weren't English, but looked like some other language's version of cursive. Though she stood next to the guy wearing the crown, there were at least two feet of distance between them, and her posture was stiff.

Guess she didn't want to be there.

Her eyes fixated on me though, and there was curiosity within them.

"The Tamed King emerges," Calian drawled. "Suppose you couldn't wait any longer to meet my female, could you?"

The man said nothing, only staring at us with narrowed eyes.

"I'm sure you've come with the desire to take Lian's new mate," the phoenix guy, Ervo, said calmly. "As you know, we'll refuse. What's the compromise you came to offer?"

My gaze skimmed all of the men on the other side of the room. There was only one I didn't recognize, so I figured he was the one who had been with Druze and Ana, trying to deal with their *human problem*.

One man spoke for their king. "Give us the rest of the females, and we'll allow your connection."

My eyebrows shot upward.

Was he serious?

There was a moment of silence.

"If your people were going to be drawn to their scents, it would've happened by now," another unseelie said coolly. "We deserve the chance to see if they're ours, same as your people."

None of the seelies said anything, and I felt multiple sets of eyes on me.

"We have yet to prove whether or not a mate bond can occur in time," Teris, the sabertooth guy in our group, said. "You've been with your human for nearly two decades, yet yours still hasn't settled the way Lian and January's has, so who can say that the connection doesn't take time?"

The king's nostrils flared, but he remained silent.

My mind was frozen on the part where the seelies weren't sure if a mating bond could develop over time. If they could... then Mare and the other girls might want to stay in the seelie part of the kingdom.

Lian had told me to listen and go with my gut, so...

It was time to lie.

"One of the other human girls confided in me already that she's felt drawn to one of the seelie fae for a few months now. We're pretty sure that a bond can come on slowly." I rattled off that bullshit like I was the best liar ever, even though I wasn't fantastic at it. "If you take them, you might break the beginning of a bond, as well as make the women furious enough to refuse to consider the rest of you at all."

Now, I had every eye in the room on me.

"She has a fair point," the other human girl admitted. "And we've all seen the bond growing between Druze and Ana on our side of the world, even if they both refuse to admit it exists."

My gaze jerked to the blond unseelie who had come to pick up the fireball of a woman when I first arrived in Vevol.

A tense moment of silence followed her admission.

"The balance of power is unsteady," the unseelie king finally said, his voice low and growly. "The seelie must give us something to steady the scales."

"Your land has far more mated couples than ours," Priel, our hellhound guy, growled back. "As you well know. If your females don't like you enough to screw you, even for the security of a bond, then you don't deserve the power anyway."

All of the unseelies' eyes narrowed at him.

"Your opinions mean nothing to us," the king finally said. "The imbalance remains. Give us the rest of the women, or we go to war."

Bastards.

The woman beside the king looked pissed. "No." Her voice was clipped, and one look at her proved she was trying her damndest to keep from losing her temper. "We do *not* want war. I'll talk to the other mated women, and one of us will have sex with our mate so that both sides have a couple with a complete bond. No one needs to die."

I looked at the girl with new eyes after she'd said that.

She was... sacrificing herself? Or one of the other mated human chicks?

Classy, if she was the one making the sacrifice.

Shitty, if she wasn't.

"Make sure only one of you does it or we'll be the ones calling a war," Priel, our hellhound, growled.

The woman dipped her head in a nod. "That's not going to be a problem." Her voice was clipped, and from what I had heard, she had a damn good reason for it.

"Is that all?" Lian asked, looking around the room and pulling me closer.

"For now." The unseelie king still studied us with a heavy, dark gaze.

"January?" The woman spoke up as Lian started to turn me away from everyone, to lead me out in front of him.

I glanced over my shoulder at her, and met her slightly-troubled gaze.

"Are you okay?" she asked, her voice low. "No one's forced you to do anything?"

My judgment of her was officially leaning toward classy. I'd put money on her being the one to seal the deal with her mate, even if she didn't want to. A shitty sacrifice, but one I could definitely respect her for making.

"I'm fine. If anyone tried to force me, I'd cut their dick off," I tossed back.

Her lips curved upward slightly. "We need to get all of the ladies together one of these days."

"Good luck getting past all these assholes." I gestured with my head toward the group of male fae flooding the room.

Her lips lifted further as she dipped her head in a nod.

I nodded back before slipping outside, with Lian's hand still gripping my waist in a comfortingly-possessive way.

"You did better than I could've hoped for," Calian murmured into my head. It had been so long since he spoke to me through the bond that I shuddered a bit at the feel of it.

"Do you guys have meetings like this a lot?" I wondered. *"Mostly pointless?"*

His chuckle was silent, but his fingers stroked the skin beneath my hip bone. *"The unseelie would never admit it, but they have a dramatic streak wider than the damned sky. They attempt to use it to force us to follow them a few times a year."*

Damn.

"So this is just a normal day in Vevol?" He must've been able to hear my question, and his lips curved up in response.

"It is. Though usually, one of the unseelies will be bleeding when we leave. They love pissing off Priel."

My lips formed a small grin. *"He seems like he might be just as dramatic as they are."*

"Oh, he is." Lian shot me a grin that mirrored my own, before he pulled me close and shifted forms.

My magic thrummed too excitedly to protest his hold on me, so when I started to shift, I did so on Calian's back. He flashed me a sharp-toothed smirk when I almost fell off, unused to balancing my huge-ass bird-self.

"You're stunning," he told me, his voice soft and sexy.

"Or are you just stunned?" I countered.

His scaly forehead sort of wrinkled.

"It was a rhetorical question, so I didn't expect you to answer."

The wrinkle on his forehead didn't budge, so I tried to explain.

"It's like the saying, 'beauty is in the eye of the beholder.' Everyone's definition of attractive is different, so calling someone or something beautiful is a waste of time. It doesn't matter if the girl in the cell next to yours is even filthier than you are; what matters is that they were stunned by her. They found her beautiful, and it worked to her advantage. You told me I was stunning, and I replied that in actuality, you were stunned by me."

A low chuckle traveled through our bond. *"To me, you are the most beautiful thing in both of our worlds. Is that a better compliment?"*

The fire on my feathers and wings grew a little hotter. For some reason, it felt nice. *"It is."*

"Do you still wish to go to my mountain?" His voice was firm enough that I knew he wanted me to say yes, but soft enough that I knew he wouldn't be upset if I said no.

There was no pressure either way, which left me with the chance to give him the truth.

"I do," I admitted.

He flashed me a slow grin over his shoulder, his ginormous teeth glinting a bright white. *"I'll race you there."*

A laugh burst out of me as the dragon rolled sideways, knocking me off his back. My wings spread through the sky, the wind forcing them open as the massive appendages kept me upright.

I glided below Calian for a moment. *"Ready?"* he asked, his voice a bit wicked.

"Yup." It was silly—I knew he was going to win, and he did too. But the adrenaline was still there, and the idea still made me ridiculously happy.

As we took off toward his mountain, flying harder than I ever had before, I admitted to myself that for the first time in the entirety of the life I could remember, I was happy.

Eighteen

THE THRILL HAD COOLED off by the time we made it back to his cave, and then I was just sort of uncertain.

All of this was new for me. The world, the magic, the mating thing...

He hadn't known what he wanted from me or with me the last time we'd talked about it, but I was pretty damn sure that had changed.

And now, we were going to be alone in his cave. On his mountain.

I landed beside him, still shifting slower than he did. It would be a long-ass time before I could change as fast as he could, but I didn't mind.

In fact, I kind of looked forward to it.

When we were both in our skin again, his gaze slowly moved up and down my body. Whether he was checking me out or just checking me for injuries was debatable, but I didn't want to wonder about it.

"I never had the chance to show you around," he remarked, lifting his gaze from my chest. "May I?" He held an elbow out to me, and my heart squeezed.

I was totally screwed.

And not just in a fun way, either. Because I wanted to be near him as much as he wanted to be near me, which was kind of terrifying.

I took his elbow anyway, fighting off the wild emotions rummaging in my abdomen.

"You mentioned a cell, before we took to the air," he said as we walked.

My stomach squeezed further.

This was getting stressful.

I needed to kiss him, or screw him, or... bail.

The urge was overwhelming, but I ignored it.

"I was in juvie. There was... someone tried to hurt me. I killed them. It wasn't an accident. It landed me in jail for a few years." The words tumbled from my lips in short, choppy sentences.

"Your people imprisoned you for protecting yourself?" His voice was low, and I heard anger lining it.

"They thought I could've protected myself less violently. I probably could've. Really, I only went to jail because the man I killed had been friends with the people who decided whether or not I'd be punished." My voice was quieter. "I don't like to think about it. Or talk about it."

"I understand." His words were gravelly, though, and I could feel his fury seeping through the bond.

Something about the anger he felt toward them made me feel more justified in my own. It made me feel kind of loved.

"In our world, you never would have suffered for choosing to protect yourself. In the unseelie packs, perhaps, but not here. Here, we are free."

I bit my lip and nodded, those wild emotions in my chest only swelling higher.

The pressure of the serious conversation was starting to overwhelm me, though, and I began to feel a little trapped.

"Here we are." Lian's words had my gaze lifting off the dirt beneath my feet. Surprise raised my eyebrows as I took in the beauty in front of me.

Nestled between the rocks and trees was a lake with a thick, slow-flowing waterfall leading down into it. It was twice the size of Calian in his dragon form—so pretty damn big—but something about it looked cozy and comfortable. The water was a vibrant blue color that reminded me of a more muted version of some of the trees.

"Shit," I murmured.

It was the kind of place that normal girls would pin pictures of on Pinterest for, of their dream vacations, and the kind of place that rich people would create those pins about.

It was incredible.

"This is yours?" I looked at Calian.

"The land belongs to all of us." He lifted a shoulder lightly, his lips curving up. "But no other fae walk onto this mountain without my permission. To do so would be a death sentence."

"So yes, it's yours." I stared back at the lake. "Is the water warm?"

"Not on its own. But I think between our magic, the two of us can heat it fairly quickly."

My lips curved up at that.

He was right; we couldn't get cold without our fire turning itself on and warming us up. If we were in the water, it would do the same to the lake.

"It's safe to swim in?" I checked.

To answer my question, Calian swept me up off my feet and threw me in. A scream escaped me as I fell into the water—and then I gasped and kicked upward as the icy lake engulfed me.

The fae grinned massively when I surfaced, as he strode into the water himself. He'd dropped his pants, which didn't surprise me for a second, considering how much I knew he didn't like the fireproof clothing.

I tried not to stare at his erection.

Despite his nudity, I knew he wasn't coming into the water to have sex with me. If steamy shit happened, neither of us would protest, but that didn't seem like the reason he'd brought me there.

He'd brought me there because it was beautiful, and because he wanted to share it with me.

"Bastard," I yelled at him, even though the water was warming up around me already, and I was fighting a grin. My soaked hair stuck to my neck until the place it met the water, and from there, it flowed around me. It was its typical color, not having changed when my magical tattoos appeared.

And said tattoos glowed lightly under the water, catching my attention and widening my grin.

"You were thinking too seriously. The land insisted I take care of it," Lian tossed back. He dove under the water, surfacing again only a few feet in front of me, grinning broadly. "I've missed having you to myself, Ari."

Something about the way he used my old nickname made my grin widen. "You've missed having me naked in your arms, you mean."

He chuckled. "That too."

My eyes closed as the water around me warmed further. It was blissful. "You never taught me to connect with my land magic," I told him, opening my eyes a few moments later. The man was staring at me without an ounce of shame, his attention never wavering.

"Come over here and I will."

Touché.

I bit back the urge to distance myself from him, to put space between us and protect myself from whatever future pain could come of it, and swam toward the man.

He caught me in his arms, pulling me to his chest. My legs wrapped around his waist, and he didn't have a problem keeping us both above the surface of the water.

"Connecting with Vevol is easy," he murmured to me, his arms wrapping around my lower back. His grip was steady, and that calmed me despite my racing heart. "Just close your eyes and feel."

That didn't make a drop of sense, but I closed my eyes anyway.

"Everything in my world has come naturally to you, as if this place was created for you and you for it." Lian's voice was a soft stroke to my spine, moving along with his hands.

I pushed away the emotions that responded to both his words and his touch, and tried to *feel* it.

Water was engulfing most of my skin, and I could feel both of our magic thrumming within it. Beside the magic, there was something else.

Something... more.

Something *alive*.

"That's it," the man holding me murmured. "Embrace it, and whisper to it. Should you ask it to do something it's willing to do, it'll follow your will."

I focused on the magic around me, not my magic or Lian's, but Vevol's. As I focused on it, I felt it focus on me in return.

"Dance," I whispered silently to the magic. It wasn't all of Vevol— it was only the part making up the water around us.

As if someone had flipped a switch, the calm water surrounding me began to move.

A laugh escaped me when it tugged us around in a small whirlpool, and I opened my eyes to watch the water come to life.

Waves built and crashed on one side of the lake, currents coming to life and whisking away portions of the water. More whirlpools formed, small, soft ones, only to turn into new currents as the old ones morphed themselves into waves and whirlpools.

"It's beautiful," I admitted to Lian, my attention fixed on the lake even though my legs were wrapped around his back and our chests were plastered together.

"Or do *you* just find it beautiful?" the fae teased.

A laugh escaped me as I turned to face him. My lips were parted, ready to tease him back for using my ideas against me, but the words died in my throat.

He was grinning at me, staring at me like I was the only thing in his world that mattered.

I couldn't help it anymore; I grabbed his face and kissed him.

His arms tightened around me as our lips moved together, our mouths parting so our tongues could find each other.

Calian's fingers tightened on my thighs as he dragged me down, nestling his erection against my core exactly the way he knew I wanted it. I inhaled sharply as his hardness pressed into me. I'd been ignoring and avoiding intimacy with him for too long; I was too needy.

We kept kissing, my core rocking against his erection. The need built hard and fast in my lower belly, but I didn't want to lose it by myself.

If I was going over the edge, I wanted to take him with me.

"I want you inside me," I ordered him mentally, so I didn't have to untangle my mouth from his.

"I want your pleasure first," he growled back.

"That can come later. Right now, I want you."

He growled at me again, aloud this time, but his fingers moved down my ass.

He didn't bother removing my shorts, just pulled the damn things to the side. The water was warm on my bare skin, and I gasped into his mouth when the tip of his cock met my entrance.

Shit, I'd forgotten how big he was.

My body throbbed with need.

"*Now, Calian,*" I snarled at him.

His sexy chuckle only heated my body further as he guided his tip into me, just an inch, while his fingers teased my clit lightly.

I groaned into his mouth when he pulled out afterward, his hands on my core, parting me and playing with me. *"Bastard,"* I moaned silently.

He slid into me again, this time a little further, holding my hips firmly as I arched so that he remained in control. The man had a dominant side, and I hated how much I loved it.

My core clenched around nothing when he pulled out again.

He slid inside me again, pulling out one more time and squeezing my ass in punishment when I tried to shove myself further onto him. Our lips separated as I cried out, my head tilting to the sky when he pulled out again. "You're mine," he growled at me, his voice a mix between possessive beast and playful tease.

"Don't torture me," I panted, my eyes closing as the desperation clutched me.

"It's preparation, not torture." He slid into me one more time, and this time, he dragged me down, and down, and down.

My words stalled in my throat, my body ceasing to function as he sheathed himself fully inside me.

He was...

And I was...

Shit, the pressure was so insanely intense.

The man was touching, *stretching*, every part of me in a way that made me dizzy with need.

He throbbed inside me once, and then again.

A low snarl built in his chest, and then he was moving us.

The pressure and fullness were so intense. I cried out as the orgasm hit me hard and fast, desperation and pleasure raising my voice as he made love to me, bottoming out and pulling back so hard and fast I couldn't take it.

One orgasm turned into another as he finally roared, shattering inside me. His throbbing took me over the edge a third time, and when I dropped my face to his shoulder, both of us were breathing raggedly.

"Dammit," I groaned into his skin. "Why are you so good at that?"

"You taught me properly, I suppose," he tossed back, breathing just as hard as I was.

It definitely wasn't just me, though. "I did *not* teach you all of that."

"You taught me how to bring you pleasure; I figured out how to do it the way I wanted to." There was both satisfaction and humor in his voice, and the emotions teased me, too.

"Well, you're good at it." My grip on him tightened.

The foster kid in me wanted to take possession of him, to tell him that if he ever so much as looked at another woman, we would be done. Or to kick in and let him know that sex was just sex—and that it wasn't anything serious.

But I didn't do or say any of that. The instincts were there, but the desire was absent.

I wanted Calian more than I wanted that emotional safety, I guessed.

"You asked me what I wanted from you, from our mating, once," Lian murmured to me. My face was still planted against his shoulder, his cock still buried inside me. "I admitted I didn't know. Now, I have no doubts."

I bit my lip, tasting the salt from both of our sweat when I did.

"I want you to be mine, in every way there is. Heart, body, soul, and mind. You have all of me; I want to have all of you as well. I know you'll need time because human relationships don't work as quickly as my people apparently prefer them to happen, and I accept that. I'll wait for as long as you wish. But as far as I'm concerned, we belong to each other, fully."

My heart swelled. "This is insane," I whispered back. "But I think I want that too. I'm not ready to proclaim my love or promise you my soul or anything, but eventually... I want that. All of it."

His lips brushed my shoulder, and then the back of my neck. I was still dressed—and my shorts were probably tugging against his erection, but he didn't seem to care.

In fact, he throbbed inside me.

"You're ready for round two?" I asked, humor in my voice.

"You say that like it's surprising." He rocked inside me just a little, and my entire body throbbed. "I'm buried inside the most beautiful woman in two worlds. Why would I not be ready for round two?"

"It's..." My mouth dried, and my whole damn body clenched when his fingers slid up my inner thigh and found my clit. He pinched me lightly, and I rocked against him.

What the hell had he done to me? I was insatiable.

"Turn me around," I rasped, my chest already rising and falling quickly.

A moment later, his hands were hot on my thighs, and he lifted me off of his cock just long enough to turn me around.

When I sank back down onto his erection, I was panting. "Shit, Lian."

"On your lips, it's Calian," he growled back at me, his fingers hot on my clit and hip as he lifted me and sank me back down, again, and again, and again.

"Calian," I repeated, my eyes closing as I focused on the sensations. Him inside me, while he played with my clit, was just too much.

I cried out as I lost it, my eyes squeezing shut as the hot pleasure coursed through me.

He snarled and went over the edge with me, throbbing inside me.

"You're incredible," I panted, dropping my head back to rest on his shoulder.

He leaned forward and captured my lips with his in response.

Nineteen

AFTER A LONG, slow, lazy kiss, we finally parted.

He slid his erection—yup, he was already hard again—out of me and fixed my shorts before he stepped around me, tugging me up onto his back. I wrapped my arms around his neck, and my chest pressed up against his ridiculously-muscular shoulders.

"What are we doing?" I checked.

"I'm going to show you something." His voice was playful again, and I loved the happiness I felt radiating off the man. It was such a simple emotion—but one I didn't think I'd ever get enough of.

He swam toward the waterfall, and I eyed it curiously. The water had gone back to its natural state at some point, so everything was quiet and calm again.

"Is it under the waterfall?" I studied the stream of water, looking for a clue that whatever he wanted to show me was hidden behind it.

"It is. Hold your breath."

I did as he instructed, and we dove beneath the falling water.

When we surfaced, I looked around in awe. There was no cave full of treasure, like I'd kind of expected given the whole dragon-and-treasure thing I'd heard fairytales about, but the cave was gorgeous. Glowing vines stretched across the walls of the space, which was twice as large as any bedroom I'd ever stayed in. A makeshift mattress of what looked like dozens of thick blankets piled on top of each other stood off to one side, with more flowers and vines growing around it, weaving the blankets together and making the bed glow.

Glittering formations of shining stone stretched down from and grew up toward the ceiling, while other bits of the stuff seemed to have dripped down the walls, creating what looked like a melted ice cream effect that made everything sparkle gorgeously.

"Damn," I murmured.

"Welcome to my mountain." The dragon gestured toward the cave. "This is the home no one but me has ever seen."

Shit, so the other cave was just to trick his brothers?

Clever.

I liked it.

"It's fireproof, I might add. The glowing flowers are called *hilsolev*, and they drop undetectable pollen that is Vevol's way of preventing fire from destroying anything beautiful."

"Nature's fire extinguisher," I murmured, looking around.

Knowing that Calian and I couldn't destroy the room, no matter how kinky things got, was definitely a relief. My room had been wrecked after the last time we were together, and I was still trying to get over that.

"How did you find this place?" I wondered, still looking around. "Or did you make it?"

"It's a long story." Calian flashed me a small grin.

"I have plenty of time."

He grabbed my hand. With a quick tug, he towed me to the bed. "Snuggle with me, and I'll tell you."

It had been a long time since we'd been in bed together.

Too long.

And even if I wanted to, I couldn't have resisted the damn snuggling.

I nodded, and he pulled me down onto the makeshift mattress with him. My clothes were already dry, thanks to their strange nature and my own heat.

We got comfortable in the bed together, with me lying on my back while Calian was propped up on his side beside me. I rested my head on one of his biceps, and his free hand sprawled over the part of my abdomen that my clothing left exposed.

"A long, long time ago, our world was almost destroyed. No one knows precisely how it happened, or how close we were to destruction. I assume that's when we lost our female fae, but no one truly knows." His fingers stroked my abdomen as he spoke. "The unseelie and seelie were already divided then, but we worked together to create the valley separating our lands to prevent more fighting after a particularly gruesome war. I was injured and set out to find a place to call my own for a time, as did the rest of the seelie. I stumbled across the cave you slept in the last time you were here, and stayed there while I healed."

His hand continued stroking my abdomen as he continued talking. "Many of our people were lost. Some, I was very close to.

Life felt very bleak. When I no longer wanted to be alone in my cave, I wandered around the mountain. As I wandered, I found the lake and took a swim. While I was swimming, I felt drawn to the waterfall, and beneath it, I found this cave. It felt like the land's whisper to me that all was going to be well in the end—and that Vevol heard me, so I wasn't alone. Things were still lonely at times, as I suppose they are for everyone, but this place was a constant reminder that our land watches out for its people to the best of its ability."

Surprise and wonder mingled in my mind at his story. "That's kind of amazing."

He made a noise of agreement, continuing to stroke my abdomen. His fingers had nudged my top up a little, exposing more skin, and I sure as hell didn't mind.

"What was life like for you after that?" I asked, curious. "Things here seem so... simple."

"They are simple," he admitted. "We create fights just to prevent ourselves from going insane at times. We have books to read, and some of our people found ways to take movies and other entertainment from your world, but we lack purpose. The moment I caught your scent on Earth, I knew everything was going to change—and I couldn't wait."

My throat swelled a bit.

"What was life like for you on Earth? From what you've said, it doesn't sound pleasant."

Well, he was right about that.

And I didn't want to tell him the truth, at first. Didn't want to acknowledge the shitty life I'd survived.

But... he was holding me.

I was in his cave, his sacred, secret place.

And as crazy as it was, I trusted him.

So, I forced my instincts to leave me the hell alone, and I told him.

"It was hard. I told you about juvie. Before that, I had no parents. No one to raise me. No one wanted me or loved me. I was just... in the way. I guess that's probably why I push you away; I'm always afraid I'll lose everything and everyone again, or that it will all end up being a lie. I didn't have a real home or a job I enjoyed. It took everything I had just to survive on Earth. Here, things are simpler. Softer. Nicer, I guess, as crazy as that sounds when you consider that the people in this world turn into monsters."

Calian's hand caressed my abdomen and ribcage. At some point, my top had slid up to rest just below my tits. "I'm sorry," he said, his voice low. "I wish I could've retrieved you from your world earlier, saved you from some of that heartache sooner."

"Thank you." My words were barely above a whisper.

The air in the room felt heavy and tense, and I wanted to fix that. To distract myself from my painful thoughts, to... go back to the ease we had shared before.

So, I slid my hand up Calian's thigh.

The man stilled as I carefully ran my fingers over his balls.

His hand moved further up my shirt, and I bit my lip when he found one of my nipples.

"Tell me of your happiest Earth memory," the man growled at me, gripping my breast before sliding his hand down and pinching my nipple between his fingers. I rocked a little, my body responding naturally to his touch as I dragged my fingers upward and wrapped them around his cock.

"You don't want to know."

He pinched my nipple, hard. "Tell me, January."

The use of my name kicked its accompanying magic into gear, and the words came out before I could stop them. "The first time I had sex with a human guy. It wasn't good sex—he was shitty. But no one could stop me, or force me to do something else. It felt like taking control of my life for the first time."

A low growl escaped him. "Tell me how he touched you."

"No." His words surprised me, and mine surprised me just as much. "I like what we have, Lian. I don't want my past to taint it."

He growled at me again, his hand sliding out of my shirt and then down my abdomen. My whole body clenched when his hand slipped into my pants. His fingers slowly dipped into the wet heat of my core.

I inhaled sharply when he dragged his finger over my clit. My fist clenched around his cock, but he didn't even flinch. Two orgasms in a row could do that to a man, I supposed.

"I want to know exactly how every man has touched you," he said, his voice low as he continued fingering me. "So I can erase your memory of their hands on your skin and replace it with my own."

"Possessive, huh?" I managed to ask, my body clenching and rocking as he rolled my clit between his fingers. A hiss escaped me when he pinched it hard.

"Extremely."

I closed my eyes. "I don't remember everything."

"Don't lie to me, January." His voice was lower, his snarl fiercer. "Tell me how they touched you."

A groan escaped me. "The first time, we were under bleachers. People were around, above us. It made it more thrilling. He was grabby. Too needy. He—" A sharp inhale cut me off. "Shit, Calian. Easy." He'd pinched my clit again, and it hurt in a way that made me dripping wet.

"Continue." His command had my back arching.

"He barely touched me before he pulled my pants down, and only licked me for a second. When I moaned, he thought I'd orgasmed, and pulled his cock out. Wore a condom." I panted, gasping between every word as Calian buried his face between my thighs and devoured me. "It was over fast. Not pleasant. I wished I'd waited for someone I loved."

Calian spread my legs wider, and his fingers slid inside me. I cried out a moment later, tightening on his fingers as I lost control.

We were both panting when he lifted his face from between my thighs, his mouth trailing over my hip and up my body.

When his erection was between my thighs, he stopped and lowered his face so his nose rested against mine. "You belong to me." His voice was low and dangerous. "Right, January?"

I was so turned on that I couldn't even think straight. "Right," I breathed.

He pushed inside me, and I cried out at the intensity of feeling all of him inside me again.

Shit, I would never get used to the insane thrill of it.

"Forget your bleachers. No one has ever, or will ever, touch you like I have," he told me, his chest rising and falling as our eyes remained locked together. "It's you and me now, January."

"You and me." I panted the words out as I moved with him.

We lost ourselves to the pleasure, then, growing silent as we worked each other until I was screaming and he was erupting inside me.

When we were both satiated, we collapsed into the position we'd been in a few minutes earlier.

"I want to hear the rest of your stories," he told me, his voice low. "I don't want any secrets between us."

"Fine," I breathed, my heart still beating rapidly. "But I told you, none of them were good. You're incredible."

"And possessive." His voice was growly. "I will make you mine in every way any other man has done it, and a million more."

Damn, that was a turn-on.

"Your funeral," I whispered back.

He chuckled, and his hand landed on my abdomen. "Tell me more about your childhood."

My throat swelled.

I didn't want to talk about it, but I could understand why he asked. And honestly, it had felt good to get some of that shit off my back with him earlier.

So I opened my mouth, and I told him everything he wanted to know.

TWENTY

SOMETHING about that cave felt magical. It felt... safe. When I told Calian about my life, it didn't feel like I was breaking my walls down; it felt like opening myself up to the possibility of love.

We could've been in there for days or weeks, talking, screwing, and laughing together. I loved every moment of it—especially the ones where he pulled out that damn pleasure-spice and rubbed it over way too many of our body parts. But eventually, we slipped out of the cave and into the water. After swimming around for a while, cleaning ourselves off, we got out and took to the skies.

Lian and I spent the better part of a day flying, trading stories, and teasing each other through our mental connection. It was, honestly, blissful.

When we grew tired, we flew back to the Stronghold. The forest around it was loud, and packed full of fae, but I knew that all of them had accepted that Calian and I were together.

I stumbled into Calian after shifting—mostly because he'd tugged me into his arms. My front was plastered to his, and I flashed him an annoyed look while he smirked at me. "Too many male eyes around here."

I went on my tiptoes to peek over his shoulder, and saw the forest legitimately *full* of fae dudes. "Holy shit."

There were four messy lines of men waiting, and it didn't take me long to figure out what the lines were for.

Each of the unmated chicks.

A snort escaped me when I saw that each of the men was holding a cake or something similar.

"I'd say news spread about the fact that mate bonds can form slowly," Calian drawled.

I couldn't even see the front of the lines, where the entrance to the Stronghold was.

"And the news that sex is a thing," I countered.

His lips lifted in a feral grin. "That too."

I smacked him on the arm, though I was grinning too. I'd never in my life smiled as often as I had during my time with Calian.

We made our way through the crowd, Calian's hand on my ass to keep me somewhat covered as he carried me. Whoever didn't move out of our way, my fae shoved with his shoulder or a wayward hand.

By the time we made it there, Calian was swearing under his breath.

"Move or lose your damn head," he growled at the last few fae in the doorway. Luckily for them, they stepped aside.

He threw the door open. To my surprise, the damn thing wasn't even locked.

We found the other members of the Wild Hunt in the living room. My eyebrows lifted as Calian carried me past all of them without so much as a greeting.

Sunny gave a wolf-whistle as she got an eyeful of my man's ass, and I caught a glimpse of Dots reaching over to cover her eyes, even though she was also grinning and checking Calian out.

My bedroom door closed hard, and I heard a couple of growls and snorted laughs from the other room.

"I can get my own clothes," I told Lian as he set me on the bed and strode into the closet.

"Of course you can." He returned with the clothing and a grin. "But it's much more enjoyable when I get them."

He tugged my shirt over my head, taking plenty of time to play with my tits in the process. When he pulled the shorts up my legs, I rolled my eyes as he did the same with my ass.

"So damn gorgeous," he growled into my mind. *"And all mine."*

"Your possessiveness seems to be getting worse, not better," I drawled back.

"It's definitely getting worse. And I expect it will continue to do so as I continue to realize how lucky I am." He leaned in and captured my mouth with his. It had been too long since we'd been together, and after that long flight, I wanted him.

But there were people in the other room, and I still didn't know whether or not the girls needed anything from us. There had to be a reason they'd let all the wild hunt guys in, right?

"After we've figured out what's going on, we'll head back to the mountain," Lian growled to me, out loud that time, as he ended the kiss. "And then I'll hold you captive for a few more days. Maybe a few more weeks."

A snort escaped me. "I don't think it counts as holding me captive when I'm there willingly."

"You can play along." His grin grew wicked.

I couldn't help but return it.

"Put your pants on before I get too horny," I complained, reaching out to grab his erection.

"Too late." He dragged my mouth toward him with a hand on my cheek, and I parted my lips to take his cock. Teasing him with my tongue a few times, I sucked a little just to make him harder.

When I pulled away, I tilted my head back. "Hurry up. The sooner we get this shit figured out, the sooner we can get back to our love cave."

He snorted. "Love cave?"

"It's the perfect name. I'll break your nose if you argue."

A laugh escaped him. "Love cave it is."

He stepped into his pants, and when I handed him one of his muscle-tees with a threatening stare, he tugged that on over his head. Once he was dressed, his hand caught mine and towed me back to my feet.

We made it out of the room and found everyone right where we'd left them.

Mare was pacing the kitchen, her hands tucked into the pocket of her massive sweatshirt. Sunny and Dots were sitting on the couch together, and Dots kept eyeing Sunny like she was afraid she was going to have to grab her or something. North was nowhere to be seen—so in her room, I assumed.

Priel, the hellhound guy, was sprawled across one of the couches, wearing an amused smirk. Ervo, the phoenix, sat on the armrest of a couch, his expression as serious as the damned grave. Teris, the sabertooth, was leaned up against the wall beside the window, his eyes scanning the lines of men as if he was waiting for someone to do something wrong. And Nev, the basilisk, was sitting on a couch of his own, staring at Sunny and Dots. I couldn't tell which of the women he was really staring at, but I supposed it didn't really matter if there was no mate-like attraction between them.

"What happened?" Calian asked everyone in the room.

"You decided that mate bonds can occur over time," Sunny said, lifting an eyebrow at Calian. "Didn't think that news would get around? You fae bastards have nothing to do but run around and gossip."

I bit back a snort.

It was kind of true.

"Best we could do to get the seelies under control was make them line up." Priel shrugged lazily, still grinning. "The unseelies have taken to sending letters."

"Letters?" My eyebrows shot to my forehead.

Mare grabbed a thick stack of them off the counter and held them up for me. "Look. Now that they know about sex, and that bonds can form over time, every one of these bastards wants us."

"Almost every one," Sunny corrected, tossing a hand toward Priel. "I already hit on that one. He's not interested."

Priel snorted. "Don't need pity sex, thanks. Pretty sure it would mate us, anyway, and I'm not interested."

Mare scowled at him. "This is serious. These people aren't looking for sex, they're looking for permanent attachments. Relationships. Love. We need to figure out a way to get them to calm down and just... leave us alone."

"Our people have been alone for a long time." Calian's voice was steady. "The only way you'll get them off your back is by mating with someone else. Even if sex wasn't on the table, they would still be here. We have no purpose right now; a mate gives us purpose."

"Lian's right. The other fae aren't leaving unless they know you're mated or you agree to see them," Nev said, still staring at Dots or Sunny. "There is an alternative, though."

"What is it?" Dots asked. "I like cake, but I don't need a couple *hundred* of them."

"The same thing we've all realized, I'm sure," Ervo spoke for Nev. "You all start bonds with us."

There was a moment of thick, stunned silence.

"We *what*?" Mare practically yelled.

"I already *tried* propositioning one of you." Sunny shot Priel a dirty look, and he lifted his hands in surrender.

"How would we even start bonds?" Dots protested. "We've gone on little dates with most of the guys out there; if we were interested or potential mates, we would've realized it by now."

"You've talked to them, but you've never touched them," I said. It was the first thing I had to offer to the conversation, but I did know more about having a mate than any of the other ladies in the room. "Kissing would probably be enough to start it. Snuggling, maybe."

All of the girls stared at me.

Mare looked like she thought I was crazy.

Sunny was grinning.

Dots seemed to be considering it.

"Absolutely not," North snarled from the doorway of her room. She turned her glare to the man beside me. "They call you their king. Send them away, and they'll listen."

"That's not how the seelie work," I answered for Calian. "The unseelie call him their king because they're trying to fit us in a box, but we don't fit. We're free. If he goes out there and tells them to leave, they'll fight him for the chance to stay. And there are enough of them that they'll eventually overpower him."

"This is on us," Dots agreed, though her voice was slightly reluctant. "We've got to build bonds if we want them to stop bringing us cake."

"I'm on board." Sunny shrugged. "Ever since I heard how much January enjoys screwing her fae, I've been on board."

A snort escaped me. "Classy."

"Just like you." Sunny winked at me.

She had a point, and we exchanged grins.

"Fine, I'll do it." Mare's face was looking a bit ashy, but her eyes were steely. "I don't want to go to the unseelies next year anyway."

All of us looked at North.

She still stood in her doorway, her fists clenched as she glowered at us.

"You don't have to do this," I told her. "But they're not going to stop coming for you if you don't, so it's a chance to take your life into your own hands."

Her jaw clenched; I saw the slight shift through her hair.

Another tense moment passed before she finally ground out, "Fine. I'm not getting with him though." She pointed a finger at Priel, who lifted his hands in surrender, still grinning.

"We'll draw names. I'm not doing a schoolyard pick," Sunny said, folding her arms over her chest. "Been there, hated that."

"We should get a veto, at least," North snarled.

Mare cut in. "No. Whichever name you draw, you get. If there's no choice involved for some of us, there's no choice involved for any of us. Otherwise, it's not fair for us or the men."

It took a moment, but finally, nods went around the room.

I didn't say a word, because I wasn't really involved in it. I'd already found my mate; neither of us was about to get roped into a fake mating.

"Fine." North gritted the word out. "January sets it up, so there's no bias."

I was actually kind of flattered that she trusted me enough not to be biased in favor of the other women.

Another round of nods circled the room.

"Here." Mare went over to one of the bookshelves and pulled out a few sheets of paper and a marker. I tugged Calian to the kitchen with me, taking the stuff too.

"Are the guys drawing the girls' names, or girls drawing guys?" I checked, as I tore the paper into four pieces.

"Girls are drawing." Sunny didn't hesitate.

The others agreed, so that was that.

Calian retrieved a bowl for me, and when North growled at him that he wasn't allowed to be involved, he stepped around to the other side of the counter and waited with the other guys. He didn't seem offended by her growl—only amused.

The whole thing seemed to amuse him though, and I had to admit I felt a little of the same. If I were in the other ladies' position, I wouldn't have found it funny though, so I kept my humor on the down-low.

I wasn't sure how to spell their names and didn't want to piss my dyslexia off, so I had the guys all write their names out a piece of paper, and then I folded each of the papers twice and put them in a bowl.

"Who's first?" I checked, shaking it up and stirring the papers around with my hand.

"This is a really messed-up Secret Santa game," Sunny muttered.

"Me." North held her hand out.

"No one opens them until we all have one," Mare warned, as I carried the bowl over to North.

She glared into the bowl, studying the papers before finally grabbing one and stepping back.

The other girls didn't care about the order, so I went to Mare, Sunny, and then Dots.

The air in the room was so thick it was hard to breathe.

Without a vocal instruction, they all opened them at once, staring down at the papers.

Not gonna lie, my heart was beating pretty damn hard. Mostly out of excitement. Also, because I was nervous for all of them.

North crumpled her paper and dropped it on the ground before turning and storming back into her room.

The door slammed so hard the damn thing rocked.

"Ervo," Mare said, biting her lip as she lifted her paper so we could see the names.

"Nev," Dots said, lifting hers too.

"Teris." Sunny followed suit.

Which left North with Priel.

...Who was currently grinning like a demon, of course.

"Let's get this over with." Sunny strode across the room and stepped in front of Teris, who was still facing the window. Then she placed her hands on his shoulders, leaned in, and kissed him.

"Can we talk in my room for a minute?" Dots asked Nev.

He dipped his head in a nod, standing smoothly when she did and then following her across the space.

Mare was biting her lip hard.

When I glanced back at Sunny, I found her and Teris still kissing—though they seemed to have graduated into an intense makeout session.

"We're gonna go..." I grabbed Calian's hand, tugging him toward my bedroom, towing him behind me. I shot Mare a thumbs-up as I went, and she gave me a panicked look in response.

There wasn't a damn thing I could do to make kissing Ervo any easier for her, though, so I shut my bedroom door behind us.

Calian grinned at me as I collapsed against the door, my shoulders shaking as I fought back laughter.

"Shh." He lifted his finger to his lips, stepping up to me so his pelvis met mine. His hands cradled my face, tipping it back and kissing me slowly and lightly. "They'll need time to talk to each other and get bonds started. When they're done, we'll address all the fae outside together. They're going to be pissed."

"Are the other guys going to have to fight?" I asked.

"I'm sure they will. They'll be thrilled about it, though. It's been too long since most of them had a real fight." His finger dragged over my lips before he leaned in and captured them.

He kissed me slowly, like he wanted to savor me.

His hands skimmed my sides, sliding down to wrap around my ass.

Our magic thrummed together, as if we were in tune with each other's power.

"You'll need to be quiet," he murmured against my lips. "Up for the challenge?"

"So damn up. Won't make a peep," I mumbled, slipping my hands under the hem of his shirt. It took a minute to work it out from under my thighs, where I'd trapped it. When it was free, I tugged it over his head, then tossed it to the ground.

He had my tank top off a moment later, and then smoothly turned me around. My tits met the door, and neither of us bothered to remove our pants.

His hand slipped into my shorts, and I clamped my jaw shut to stop myself from moaning when he stroked me, rocking his erection against my ass while he played with me. My breathing picked up, my body already hot and wet for him.

"You ready?" he growled into my mind.

"Hell yes," I panted back.

He tugged my shorts to the side. A heartbeat later, he slammed his cock into me in one hard, fluid motion. Our bodies rocked as they slapped together, and we froze for a moment, making panicked eye contact about the unintentional noise.

A snort escaped me, and he flashed me a wicked grin before he resumed. The man set a brutal pace, knowing exactly which angle was the best for me, and working my clit with his fingers at the same time.

The door shook as we made love, but neither of us cared—we were lost to the moment, to the pleasure.

I cried out into Calian's mind as I lost control, and his teeth clenched down on my shoulder as he held back his snarl. We shattered together, and as we lost it, a thought flittered across my mind.

If this wasn't love, I wasn't fucking interested.

TWENTY-ONE
CALIAN—6 MONTHS LATER

THE SOUND of flapping wings and paws on the ground met my ears as my palm slid over the smooth skin on January's back. She was asleep on the mattress in our less-friendly cave, the one she called our Home Cave. The other one, with the glowing flowers, was still the Love Cave. I didn't give a damn what she called them, so long as she slept in them with me.

And I was a lucky bastard, because she *always* slept in them with me.

Her snores were soft, her body more relaxed in sleep than it ever was during waking hours. I loved her when she was sleeping— then again, I loved her when she was awake, too.

I didn't bother with pants before striding out of the cave. My brothers were outside; I could hear them, and none of us cared if we were clothed. When you've seen one cock, you've seen them all.

They were arguing about something, but had stopped far enough from the Home Cave that they hadn't woken January, which was wise of them. If they'd woken her, I'd be pissed. When my female was tired, I wanted her sleeping. Especially considering I was the bastard who usually tired her out.

Recently, her scent had started to change. I didn't understand what the newest additions to it meant, and she said she wasn't ready to talk about it yet, but she'd started to tire easily and sleep more.

Even before approaching, I already knew what my brothers were arguing about.

It was always about the same thing, after all.

The women in the Stronghold, and the other fae who still insisted on fighting over them.

We enjoyed fighting, but six months of it nonstop was enough to wear anyone out.

"I'm not doing it anymore," Priel snarled. "I'm tired of the blood."

"What's the alternative?" Teris's weary voice countered. "Lock her in a room with you until you convince her to screw you?"

"Might as well ask one of us to kill you," Nev replied, his voice smooth and even.

Priel growled, "I'm going to throw her over my shoulder and haul her back to my cave. At least there, I have people who will keep the other bastards away long enough to get some real sleep."

"We don't need to kill him, then," Ervo mused. "North will do it for him."

They all turned to me when I reached them. "What's this I hear about abducting a female?"

"Technically, she's mine. I convinced her to kiss me, after all," Priel countered.

"You can't abduct her," Teris growled.

"Why not? Would any of you stop me?" His gaze scanned the group of us. "You know I wouldn't do anything messed up. Just take her somewhere safe so I can get a few nights' rest."

No one said anything.

His lips stretched in a wicked grin.

Damn, he was really going to do it.

"See you assholes in a few days." He didn't bother with any other pleasantries, turning and running into the forest without so much as a backward glance.

The bastard was faster than most of us; he would probably beat us there by a long shot.

But none of us made an effort to run after him.

"The bastard's idea isn't terrible," Ervo admitted, running a hand over his buzzed hair. "Maybe I'll get desperate enough eventually."

Teris shook his head. "Not worth it. Piss off one of those girls, and they'll all castrate you together."

"I can confirm that," January agreed.

My head jerked to the side, surprised to hear her voice. She was walking toward us, her arms wrapped around her abdomen. The woman was a damn goddess, having embraced the wildness of being both fae and seelie. The markings on her skin glowed, her eyes were bright, and her expression was calm. "What happened?"

"Priel's going to abduct North. Says he needs a few days of sleep," I explained as she stepped up to my side and snuggled in.

She snorted. "Bastard doesn't know what's about to hit him. That girl's going to kill him all on her own; she won't need the rest of us."

"Probably true," Teris grunted.

There was a moment of silence before January spoke up again. She was biting her lip, like she did when she was nervous, and I studied her closely.

"So, I have news," she said. "I didn't tell you guys everything about sex."

I narrowed my eyes at her.

What else could there be? We couldn't keep our hands off of each other most of the time, and she sure as hell enjoyed it at least as much as I did. I made sure of that every time, and prided myself in doing so.

"I didn't think it mattered, because none of us are human, but on Earth, if you have sex, it can lead to pregnancy."

There was a long pause.

She had me with that one.

"Women can grow babies, on Earth. Small people. They grow into bigger ones. I'm sure you've seen baby animals, on Vevol?" She looked at me, her face pinker than usual.

Was she embarrassed, or nervous?

I pulled her closer.

The other men nodded, and I realized she was waiting for confirmation, so I nodded too.

"I haven't had cycles since I've been here, so I didn't think it was possible, but..." She bit her lip again.

"Out with it," I growled at her.

She sighed. "I'm pretty sure I'm pregnant."

There was a long, heavy pause.

"Growing a baby?" I finally asked.

She dipped her head in a nod. "I won't know for sure for a few months, if I start showing, but other than not having a period, I have all the other symptoms. Exhaustion, bloating, excessive hunger... You're staring at me weird. Why are you staring at me weird?"

"This baby... it's Lian's?" Ervo asked.

She snorted. "Yes, definitely."

"And it's growing in your..." I trailed off.

"Uterus. Down here, below my stomach." She tapped her lower belly.

I sank to my knees in front of her, shock coursing through my veins.

My hands found her hips, and I leaned in toward her belly.

"Congratulations," one of the men said. "It's time we take our leave."

The other men agreed, and the forest grew silent as they left.

I was still staring at her lower belly, inhaling her changed scent. When I lifted my gaze, I found her eyes watering as she looked down at me. "You're excited?" she whispered.

"There are no words to describe my emotions." I leaned in, pressing my forehead to her abdomen. Her hands tangled in my hair.

"I was worried you'd hate me," she admitted.

My gaze lifted to hers, and then I stood smoothly, taking her in my arms and capturing her lips in mine for a long, thorough kiss. When I pulled away, I growled softly, "There's nothing in this world or the next that could make me hate you, and you know it."

Her cheeks reddened again. "Yeah." She bit her lip again, and after a long moment, admitted, "I love you, Calian. At first, I was terrified about the baby, but now... now, I'm so damn excited I can't even explain it."

I dragged her back into my arms, recapturing her lips with mine. The kiss was hot, fierce, brutal, and...

I pulled away. "You're having a *baby*?"

"*We* are having a baby," she corrected me.

My lips stretched in a grin. "And it'll resemble us both?"

"Hopefully, it'll just resemble you. But yeah, it should theoretically be a mixture of both of us."

I dragged her into my arms and took her lips again, pulling away when I couldn't stand it anymore. After tugging her shirt over her head, I tossed it to the ground near our feet. "You are everything I never dared dream for myself, and so much more."

Her shorts followed, and I kneeled in front of her, staring up at her.

Her knees shook a bit. "Right back at you, big guy."

I snorted, and her lips stretched into a wide grin.

My chest was so warm I thought it might burst.

I grabbed her by the ass, parting her legs and taking her weight as I dragged her core to my lips, kissing her until she fell apart in my arms.

When she was dripping wet, with dilated eyes, and was panting like she'd flown around the whole damn world, I laid her down on her back and lowered myself over her.

"You are my everything," I told her again, my voice rough and gravelly as I positioned myself against her slit. "And so much more."

Her eyes watered as I slid inside her.

The whole world could've been staring at us as we made love on our mountain, but neither of us cared.

We were together.

We were *one*.

And that was all that mattered.

EPILOGUE
NORTH

MY MUSIC PLAYED loud enough to drown out the sounds of the men fighting outside. The northern wall of my bedroom was covered in wet paint; its newest mural was a gruesome picture of fire, hellhounds, and death.

That was all I saw.

Myself, burning.

Priel, burning.

All the hounds in this world, burning.

And me, at the center of them.

It wasn't any kind of future-sight, as far as I knew. I wasn't some type of oracle. My brain was just really damn twisted.

There was a knock at my door.

"I'm not hungry," I snarled at whoever was there.

I felt bad for snarling, but not bad enough to chill. If they came in, they'd see the evidence of my dreams and nightmares all over the walls. Some of them knew that I painted, but most of them didn't. I didn't really care whether they knew or not, anyway.

There was a loud crack, and then my locked door swung open.

I was on my feet in an instant, my eyes burning as I snarled at the person in the doorway.

Only, it wasn't someone who would fear my fire.

It was the hellhound who haunted my dreams—and not just the nightmares. If I had one more sex dream about the bastard, I was going to burn my bed on *purpose*.

"Get out," I roared at him.

"No can do." He crossed the room, stalking toward me like a damn predator.

I didn't step back. "Don't touch me," I spat.

"Sorry, love. Got to get some rest." With that, he grabbed me by the waist, threw me over his shoulder, and took off out the door.

Shit, I was screwed.

READ NORTH & Priel's Story Now

Afterthoughts

A few months before I started this book, I felt like total garbage. I was burnt out, I'd started resenting my writing, and I just needed a break. I ended up taking almost two months off—which is an insane amount of time for someone who writes as quickly and as much as I do.

But it ended up being one of the best things I ever did for my mental health.

Anyway, this does pertain to this story, I promise. Because while I wasn't writing, I was thinking, and this one quote by Steve Jobs kept coming to my mind. You don't really know me, most likely, but I'm a quote person. I'm sort of obsessed.

Anyway, the quote is, "You are already naked. There is no reason not to follow your heart."

Maybe you're scratching your head now, but I'll keep explaining because I'm already stuck in the mental vomit.

No, I'm not writing naked (though that would be kind of kinky?). But something about writing a book and publishing it, putting it out there for people to judge and hate or love and obsess over, feels a lot like stripping yourself naked. You're putting something that came from your mind, from your soul, up on a stage and just *letting* people throw rocks at it, or hearts, or whatever the hell else they want to throw at it.

It feels like being naked.

And that's terrifying.

Honestly, it's why I needed the time off.

But as I thought about this quote, I realized my problem.

I'd been stripping myself naked by publishing so many books, *writing* so many books, and I wasn't following my heart. I was writing trilogies, because that was what most of the other authors that I wanted to be like were selling. I was ignoring the panic that hit me every time I got to book two, or book three. I was ignoring the longing to focus on other characters in the series.

And it wasn't what I wanted to do.

I still love the books I wrote that way, and I definitely always will.

They're pieces of me; they're my book babies!

But for me to be sitting back down and writing again after the mental shittery I was dealing with a few months ago, I have to be done trying to follow other people's lead. I'm not writing to match other authors, or even to follow the market anymore.

I have to focus on writing the books that, as a reader, I want to pick up myself.

Maybe some won't be dark or twisty now.

Maybe some won't be as long.

Maybe some will be steamier.

I'll definitely be going back and forth between a few series now, so I don't get tired of my worlds.

And maybe some people will hate all of that.

But I'm the one who's naked (figuratively) and because of that, I'm going to follow my heart.

So, anyway, this book is the second that I've written that way. And this book...

It felt like it came from my soul.

And I'm truly sorry if you miss the old Lola, but that's not me anymore, and I refuse to go back to her.

Thank you for reading my books (even if this is your first). Thank you for making my dreams a reality. I still can't believe that I'm a real, actual author. My husband laughs at me every time I say it, but it's the honest truth. I still just feel like a twenty-five-year-old who's obsessed with love stories.

But I'm here.

And I'm so ridiculously happy to be back here, loving my writing again, and grinning stupidly at all of my terrible jokes.

So thank you for reading, from the bottom of my (naked) heart. I know, I know, too many dirty jokes. At least I make myself laugh with them. *shrugs*

All the love,

Lola Glass.

PLEASE REVIEW

Here it is. The awkward page at the end of the book where the
author begs you to leave a review.
Believe me, I hate it more than you do.
But, this is me swallowing my pride and asking.
Whether you loved or hated this story, you made it this far, so
please review! Your reviews play a MASSIVE role in determining
whether others read my books, and ultimately, writing is a job for
me—even if it's the best job ever—so I write what people are
reading.
Regardless of whether you do or not, thank you so much for
reading <3
-Lola

ALL SERIES BY LOLA GLASS

Fantasy Romance-

Wild Hunt Standalones

Kings of Disaster Standalones

Night's Curse Standalones

Burning Kingdom Trilogy

Sacrificed to the Fae King Trilogy

Shifter Queen Trilogy

Supernatural Underworld Duology

Paranormal Romance-

Feral Pack Standalones

Mate Hunt Standalones

Wolfsbane Series

Shifter City Trilogy

Moon of the Monsters Trilogy

Rejected Mate Refuge Trilogy

Outcast Pack Standalones

STAY IN TOUCH

Check out Lola's Facebook group,
Lola's Book Lovers,
for giveaways, teasers, and more!

Or find her on:
TIKTOK
INSTAGRAM
PINTEREST
GOODREADS

About the Author

Lola is a book-lover with a *slight* romance obsession and a passion for love—real love. Not the flowers-and-chocolates kind of love, but the kind where two people build a relationship strong enough to last. That's the kind of relationship she loves to read about, and the kind she tries to portray in her books.

Even if they're about shifters :)